Mystery boarder . . .

"You know what some people say—Dead Man's Curve got its name because some kid on a skateboard refused to bail . . . Boom! Wipeout. Permanently. Know what I mean?" Vickie asked.

"Nah," said Skate. But he did know what she meant. He'd thought about it himself. He just didn't want to tell her he had.

Vickie went on, "So the kid comes back, see? We've done something to annoy his ghost, or maybe he can't rest, and he comes back and he lures us up here."

"No, it's some high school flight master," said Skate. "Or"—he turned toward Vickie, unable to conceal his enthusiasm—"a famous boardman. He's here to practice in *secret.*"

"Yeah, right," Vickie answered sarcastically. She stopped. "Wait! Do you hear that?"

They'd just reached the boulders. From beyond came a faint *scritch-scritch*ing, like a wheel on a skateboard slightly out of sync.

"Maybe that's him!" gasped Vickie. "Let's go!"

Eager to be the first to see the mysterious skateboarder, she ran ahead of Skate into the dark on the other side of the rocks.

She half jumped, half fell back up the road, scrambling toward Skate, her eyes so wide, Skate could see the whites all around them.

"It's him. The ghost! It's himmmmm!" she screamed.

Other Skylark Books you won't want to miss!

GRAVEYARD SCHOOL

2

The Skeleton on the Skateboard

Tom B. Stone

A SKYLARK BOOK

Toronto New York London Sydney Auckland

RL 3.6, 008-012

THE SKELETON ON THE SKATEBOARD
A Skylark Book / September 1994

Skylark Books is a registered trademark of Bantam Books,
a division of Bantam Doubleday Dell Publishing Group, Inc.
Registered in U.S. Patent and Trademark Office and elsewhere.

Graveyard School   is a registered trademark of
Bantam Doubleday Dell Publishing Group, Inc.

ISBN 0-553-48224-6

Published simultaneously in the United States and Canada

Bantam Books are published by Bantam Books, a division of
Bantam Doubleday Dell Publishing Group, Inc. Its trademark,
consisting of the words "Bantam Books" and the portrayal of a
rooster, is Registered in U.S. Patent and Trademark Office and in
other countries. Marca Registrada. Bantam Books,
1540 Broadway, New York, New York 10036.

PRINTED IN THE UNITED STATES OF AMERICA

OPM   0 9 8 7 6 5 4

GRAVEYARD SCHOOL

2

The Skeleton on the Skateboard

CHAPTER

1

When he saw the graves, he knew he was dead.

He slammed his foot down on the heel of his skateboard. He swerved. His board shot out from under him and did a flip into the air.

Skate McGraw crashed hands first into an old tombstone by the side of the road at the edge of the cemetery. He heard his board clatter to a stop somewhere farther down the hill.

Then everything was quiet except for the eerie sound of the wind that always blew through the tombstones up on Graveyard School Hill.

"Wipeout," said Skate. He rolled over and saw the worn gray granite of the tombstone leaning over him. It read, REST IN PEACE.

He groaned, closed his eyes, and lay still. Maybe he would stay there forever. Maybe he'd stay there until he died.

Maybe he was dead already.

"Get up," a voice said above him.

Skate thought about it. He wiggled his toes inside his high-tops. He flexed his fingers inside their battered wrist guards. He opened his eyes. He sat up.

Vickie Wheilson stood on the road staring down at him. She was dressed in ripped jeans, an enormous purple sweatshirt, wrist guards as battered as his, scuffed orange high-tops decorated with Day-Glo magic marker and a neon green helmet.

Skate winced. He was wearing ripped jeans and a sweatshirt and a helmet and sneakers too. But his sweatshirt was gray, his helmet was plain white, and his sneakers were black.

Then Skate realized that Vickie was holding two skateboards, hers (most recently painted purple, red, and neon green) and his.

He was relieved to see that his skateboard looked okay in spite of the slam dunk he'd just given it.

"It's not even scratched," said Vickie. "Your board. Except maybe the rail guard, and that's what it's there for." She was referring to the thin strip of plastic that ran down the outside edges of the skateboard.

Studying him with intent hazel eyes, she went on. "I thought you said you weren't going to *do* Dead Man's Curve again."

Skate made a face. His cousin was a pest. And he

really didn't like the way she remembered *everything* he said.

"Right." Vickie waited while Skate got up. Then she handed him his skateboard.

"Well, you *weren't* ready," she went on. "In case you wanted to know. You might never be. You just have to face that, Skate McGraw. No one's ever made it down Dead Man's Curve standing up."

Skate sighed. Vickie always had an opinion.

The two of them looked at the hill. Above them on either side of the road, squeezing it together like a vise, a pair of huge rocks marked where the road divided. The road that went down between the rocks, past the cemetery, was called Dead Man's Curve. The road that forked off before the rocks to the right was called Skateboard Hill.

Skateboard Hill was a long, sweeping curve of old farm road that no one used anymore. It sloped gently down the far side of the hill before disappearing into the trees. On the other side of the trees it came out eventually onto Grove Road, the main road that led out of town.

Dead Man's Curve was made of angles and curves. One of the curves led directly onto a narrow, high-railed bridge above a deep, icy stream that ran through the cemetery. Beyond that bridge the road dropped with sickening steepness before curving back up another hill. Over that hill was an even steeper drop down to the old parking lot of the church that had once been there. All that was left of the church was the parking lot and the cemetery.

Skate thought, as he always did, about whether the graveyard was what really gave Dead Man's Curve its name. Or had it been something else? Someone who'd died on the curve and been buried in one of the graves beyond?

No one knew. No one ever visited the old graveyard now, not even the students who attended school in the only building left nearby: Grove School, also known as Graveyard School.

When he wasn't boarding, Skate went to Graveyard School. So did his cousin Vickie. During school Skate spent a lot of his time staring out of the classroom window.

Staring at Dead Man's Curve.

"No one's ever made it to the bottom of Dead Man's Curve *alive*," said Vickie. "Maybe you should give it up. So you can't do it. So what? There are other tricks, you know."

"Anybody can ollie a trashcan," said Skate at last. He turned and started trudging back up to the top of the hill.

Vickie stopped and put her hand on her hip. "What does that mean? I *can* do trashcans, and you know it, Skate McGraw! And I'll be doing more than that soon. You wait."

4

"You go too fast, you're gonna crash," Skate said.

"Yeah, tell me about it," answered Vickie sarcastically. "I just saw. So, are you gonna try again, or what?"

Skate shook his head. Satisfied, Vickie hurried to catch up with him. They walked the rest of the way to the top in silence.

From the top of the hill the view was awesome.

Graveyard School was on the edge of town, and except for the school and the cemetery and the few houses along Grove Road, which led past the school, the landscape below them was woods and trees and farmland. Behind them the road they called Skateboard Hill started just over the hill, back in the woods, a dirt road there that was gradually being eaten by the forest.

The road had had an official name, somewhere in time, but no one remembered it. Everyone at Graveyard School called it Skateboard Hill now.

No one ever tried to board the Curve—except Skate. Everyone else hung a right down Skateboard Hill. Skateboard Hill was a perfect skateboard ride.

But lately that hadn't been enough for Skate. He was restless. He dreamed of bigger things. He was serious about skateboarding as an Olympic event. He was serious about being the best on a skateboard in the world.

Dead serious.

Alone, long after Vickie had gone home, he practiced impossible turns and gravity-defying flights. He wanted to invent a trick so unique, so impossible that it would be named for him. A trick that would be part of an Olympic skateboarding routine someday.

But he failed. He fell. He wiped out.

He couldn't seem to get anything right no matter how hard he tried. And he was beginning to blame it all on Dead Man's Curve.

Skate settled his board and put one foot on. Behind them the sun was beginning to set. He looked down at his shadow stretched out before him. A gust of wind whipped past to join the cold wind that whined over the graveyard.

"Do you think it's true?" asked Vickie for about the thousandth time in her life. "Do you think there's a grave that glows in the dark down there?"

She didn't expect Skate to answer. He seldom did. But he was her first cousin, and she'd known him all her life, and it didn't matter anyway. She put her own board down and planted her foot. She leaned forward slightly, watching him out of the corner of her eye. She liked to get a head start on Skate, just to annoy him.

But before she could take off, Skate said, "Hear that?"

Vickie straightened up. "Hear what?"

They both listened for a long moment as the sun sank lower and their shadows grew darker on the ground. But the only sound was the wind.

Then Vickie frowned. "Yeah. That's funny," she said. "It sounds like—wheels? Skateboard wheels."

Vickie and Skate both turned and looked behind them, over the edge of the hill. But no one was riding a skateboard along the top of the hill toward them.

No one was on the hill below them either.

The sun dropped as if it had fallen off the edge of the earth. The world got darker suddenly, and colder.

"It'll be night soon," said Vickie. She didn't add that she suddenly felt creepy. That the hairs on her neck were standing on end. That a chill of goose bumps had crept up her arms.

She pushed off and headed down Skateboard Hill.

Skate pushed off behind her. He swung past her just at the entrance to Dead Man's Curve and banked toward Skateboard Hill. For a moment it seemed that the wind picked up.

"Hey," said Vickie. "Wait for me!"

Vickie followed Skate without looking toward Dead Man's Curve. She kept her eyes on Skate all the way down until the road dipped into the woods and out of sight of the old graveyard, She concentrated on the ride and not on the weird feeling that someone was watching them.

Someone. Or something.

She didn't look back once.

If she had, she would have seen she was right.

CHAPTER
2

Graveyard School was a big building with white trim and broad, shallow stairs leading up the front door. Every morning before school the students who arrived early gathered on the steps in strict order, first-graders on the bottom, sixth-graders at the top, From their places on the stairs the early kids watched the later kids arrive.

From inside, Dr. Morthouse, principal of Graveyard School, watched the students.

Skate always arrived on or with his skateboard, depending on the weather. He was often late, but he was never early. He wasn't a bad student. But he was a bored one.

The morning after his wipeout-as-usual on Dead Man's Curve, Skate raced to the bottom of the steps as the first bell was ringing and the general drift of students in the front door had begun. He tick-tacked up the stairs, front wheels of his board on the step above him, then the back, then the front wheels on the next step, then the back wheels, all the way to the top.

He looked up, pleased. He stopped.

Hannibal Lucre, the assistant principal, was standing at the school door. Mr. Lucre rubbed his plump hands together and smiled his toothy smile. He was a round man who always wore brown suits and bright-colored ties. And he always combed his mouse-brown hair in one big strand over the top of his shining bald head. He frequently ended announcements over the school's intercom with the reminder "Remember, boys and girls, I am your friend!"

Skate had once been moved to say after a Lucre announcement, "He must be hard up for friends."

Since Skate seldom spoke, that remark had made him almost as famous as his skateboard had.

But not quite.

"*Ryan,*" said Mr. Lucre now, rubbing his hands together happily. Skate didn't answer. He'd almost forgotten his real name anyway.

"We know that skateboarding isn't allowed in school, don't we, young man?"

In answer Skate stomped on the tail of his skateboard and flipped it up into his hands protectively.

Mr. Lucre backed up slightly and chuckled, "You weren't going to ride that in the halls, were you?"

Skate frowned.

Mr. Lucre waited.

Skate frowned harder.

Mr. Lucre pulled a handkerchief from his breast pocket and wiped his hands. He stuffed the handkerchief back and said, "Well, we'll let you go this time, although you really shouldn't be skateboarding on the school steps, you know. Rules *are* rules."

Mr. Lucre waited again.

Holding his skateboard close so that it didn't touch the assistant principal, Skate walked through the door into the school. He went quickly to his locker and opened it. He scraped a couple of books and a notebook out onto the hall floor and leaned the board carefully against the back of the locker. Stuffing the books in his pack, he slammed the locker and turned.

Ahead was a long stretch of smooth, empty hallway. Skate had never boarded in the school. But he'd often dreamed of it. He sighed. Seven more hours to go before he could hit Skateboard Hill.

And Dead Man's Curve.

Skate made it into his homeroom just as the last bell rang. He took his usual seat by the window and turned to stare out.

Far away the treacherous stretch of Curve was no more than a fat ribbon in the bright sunlight, winding down past the crazily tilted tombstones. The narrow bridge looked like a toy. It could have been a scene—minus the tombstones—from his little sister's picture books.

" . . . Skate McGraw," said Ms. Camp.

Skate looked up in surprise to find the whole room looking at him.

"Well, Skate, are you here today. Or not?" asked Ms. Camp, her pencil poised above her attendance book.

"Oh!" Skate paused. "Here."

A few people snickered. Perfect Polly Hannah, sitting at the front of the room with her feet together and her hands folded on her desk, said, "He *never* listens." She looked over her shoulder and glared at Skate.

Ms. Camp merely smiled and moved on. Skate liked Ms. Camp. She was decent.

He turned his attention back to the view.

Dead Man's Curve. The past summer he'd trained Dead Man's Curve. Seriously.

He'd thought he was prepared.

He'd been really psyched. He'd waxed his board, set his wheels just right. He spent the whole week before enacting the perfect run in his head, the way he heard some Olympic champions did before their big events.

But something had made him keep it a secret. He hadn't even told Vickie about it. After he'd done it, after he'd made it down the Curve, he would talk about it.

The day had been ideal for skateboarding. Warm,

not too hot, not too windy. He'd come off the top of the hill at exactly the right speed. When he'd reached the split in the road, he hadn't even been tempted to turn right down Skateboard Hill.

Still at easy speed, he made it through the rocks.

And suddenly he'd been very, very cold. The board had seemed to pick up speed of its own accord. The soles of his shoes felt as if they were sliding instead of gripping the board.

Unbalanced, he'd straightened up slightly. He still flushed at the memory of doing such a stupid thing. Straightening up had made the board that much harder to control.

The road had felt as if it had turned to glass beneath him.

He'd managed to hang on to the outside of the curve. But the sight of the bridge coming toward him at hyperspeed had been too much.

He'd bailed—also in hyperspeed—so fast that he hadn't been able to get his arms up for protection. He'd left enough skin on the road to make a twin brother, despite the jeans, high-tops, thick socks, and wrist guards he was wearing.

He'd also broken his collarbone.

He didn't remember exactly what had happened after that until he rolled over to discover that one arm was sickeningly floppy at the shoulder. Trying to ignore his arm, Skate had shakily found his board, belly-up at the edge of the bridge, its wheels spinning with a soft, sad sound.

For a moment Skate had panicked. *I've killed my board,* he thought. That hurt worse then his collarbone.

His skateboard was a truly excellent piece of equipment. To outward appearances it was plain: smooth-grained maple polished to a mellow gloss, with matching wheels, clear rail guards to protect the edges on either side of the board.

Skate gave his board respect, added custom touches now and then, and always trusted how it felt. They were partners. His board had never let him down.

Until they'd taken on Dead Man's Curve.

But maybe it *hadn't* let him down. Maybe he'd let it down, trying something he wasn't ready for.

Cradling his board, Skate examined it carefully.

He might have let his board down, but it hadn't let him down. Except for a new, slightly deeper scrape along the rail guard, it had been untouched. Reassured, Skate had folded the hurt arm up against his chest, tucked his board under his other arm, and trudged home.

His parents had gone ballistic, even though he'd been smart enough not to tell them where he'd fallen. He'd had to wear his arm strapped up for weeks, and his father had locked up his skateboard to keep him from riding it until the doctor said his collarbone was okay.

It had been the longest summer of his life.

Dead Man's Curve had seen to that.

He hadn't been the same since.

Dead Man's Curve.

Until he was able to shoot Dead Man's Curve, he was dead useless. Until he could master the curve he wouldn't be able to master anything else.

He wasn't afraid. He hadn't lost his nerve.

But he was beginning to wonder if it was true: No one ever got out of Dead Man's Curve alive.

"Ryan McGraw, please come to the office. Ryan McGraw, please come to the office."

"It's you," said Maria Medina, who sat behind Skate. She gave him a poke.

Skate looked up, surprised.

"What did he do?" asked Roy Carne as Skate walked to the front of the room to get an office pass from his teacher. "What did you do, Skate?"

Skate ignored Roy. But he had the same question himself.

What had he done?

The day had been typical: boring math, boring history, boring English, boring lunch, and now boring science—although he had been toying with an idea about doing his next science project on skateboard aerodynamics, and pondering the possibility of also doing his research project in history on the development of the skateboard.

Had Mr. Lucre changed his mind about reporting Skate for boarding on the front steps? Why had he waited until almost the end of the day to do it? But it hadn't been Mr. Lucre's voice, just the school secretary's.

For a moment Skate considered stopping by his locker and removing his skateboard. Maybe he should stash it in a safer place to be recovered later, in case Mr. Lucre had decided to confiscate it.

No. He just wouldn't let them take his board.

They'd have to expel him first. Then he could go to California and become a professional. Or start working on building the first Olympic skateboarding team.

He pushed open the office door and met the steely gaze of Mr. Kinderbane, the school secretary and office manager.

"There you are," said Mr. Kinderbane, his eyes unfriendly. He took short, snuffling breaths through his nose, as if students smelled funny to him.

Skate nodded.

"Your mother called. You have to go straight home from school today. The baby-sitter has to leave early and you have to stay with your little sister."

Skate was startled into saying, "I can't!"

Mr. Kinderbane raised his eyebrows. He sniffed. "Would you like to use the phone over there to call your mother at her office?"

Skate shook his head.

"I didn't think so," said Mr. Kinderbane. He reached out and plucked the pass from Skate's fingers, countersigned it, and gave it back to him. "You may go back to class now, Ryan. Have a nice day."

"What'dja do?" muttered Roy after Skate was safely back at his desk.

Skate shrugged. Roy was a jerk. He hung out with Eddie Hoover, the world-class jerk of the school. It annoyed Skate even to have to think about Eddie, and Roy reminded Skate of Eddie.

He stared longingly out the window at Skateboard Hill.

He narrowed his eyes. Squeezed them shut and opened them again.

For a moment he thought he'd seen someone headed down Skateboard Hill, bearing left onto Dead Man's Curve.

But no one emerged from between the boulders, no one flickered past the slat railings of the bridge.

It must have been the sun, thought Skate, hunching over his notebook. He tried not to look out the window again. Bad enough that he couldn't go out this afternoon. He didn't need to start imagining things too.

"Hey, ugly, where'ya going?"

"Hey, stupid, who're you talking to?" retorted Vickie. She flicked her skateboard off the curb and then back on, slalomed a bicycle, a tricycle, and a dog sleeping on the sidewalk, then hung some air over a wagon.

Out in the street Eddie Hoover pulled even with her on his enormous, shiny-new board. Eddie's boards were always new. He crashed them all the time. He never fixed them, never took care of them, never got to know a board. He just kept buying new ones.

He jumped the curb with a thunk and skated close to Vickie.

She ignored him. She hated Eddie with all her heart. He was a bully and a show-off. Eddie wasn't really bigger than the other kids, but he was thicker, from his thick head that was exactly as wide as his thick neck all the way down to his big, thick feet. He was also meaner.

Vickie reached back and pumped her board forward, trying to pick up speed without looking as if she were running away. She knew she couldn't outrun Eddie, but she was pretty sure she could outmaneuver him. The trick was to make it to the next block, which was a little-kid-built obstacle course of tricycles and wagons and kickballs and Nerf balls and moving objects such as little kids and their goofy dogs. She could lose Eddie there.

And Skate lived at the end of the block.

She usually took that block slow and easy. Parents were touchy when you used their kids for skateboard slaloming. But today it might be worth it. . . .

18

Eddie cruised closer. She could smell his stale pea-nut-butter breath. The brand-new shine of his board made her want to punch him right in one of his little pig eyes.

Not that she could see his eyes. Eddie was wearing the latest in wrap-around shades, like the skiers on the Olympic teams wore. He was also wearing knee pads, wrist pads, and a helmet that all matched, as well as practically new leather skateboard shoes with extra padding.

It all made him look twice as thick. And twice as mean.

Vickie tried not to look at him at all.

Instead she took a quick look both ways, jumped the curb, and crossed the street.

A million little kids were racing through the front yards ahead. Another million were tricycling furiously up and down their driveways. More little kids, even younger, playing intently on the sidewalks. From front steps and porches parents and baby-sitters watched while dogs ran around barking and chasing balls.

Eddie was so close that his shoulder brushed hers.

Vickie kicked up over the curb and onto the sidewalk and picked up the pace.

Eddie's shoulder bumped hers again. Harder this time.

Gritting her teeth, Vickie veered around an aban-doned bicycle with training wheels.

Eddie veered around the other side.

They were moving faster now. The long nose of Eddie's monster board edged out ahead. With a quick twist he turned his board in front of hers.

She'd been expecting it. Even more quickly she stomped on the heel of her board and veered past Eddie, throwing her elbow into his side as she passed for good measure.

Vickie was sorry the moment she felt her elbow connect with Eddie's thick ribs. He gave a howl. She knew what that howl meant. It meant *You are going to die.*

She began to board as fast as she could down the block, cutting between two kids drawing with chalk on the sidewalk.

Someone shouted, "Hey, slow *down.*"

She speeded up.

Behind her she could hear the heavy grind of Eddie's wheels.

If she could make it to Skate's house, she might still stand a chance, Then it would be two against one.

Eddie's board jammed hers from behind. She veered, cutting him off so he couldn't come up next to her.

"Watch out!" a voice screamed.

Two kids on bicycles with training wheels were just coasting out of a driveway onto the sidewalk. To one side of the driveway was a hedge of rosebushes. To the other side was a fire hydrant.

Vickie veered toward the rose hedge. Thorns raked her sleeves.

"Move!" she screeched at the two kids.

The kids on the bicycles looked up. They saw Vickie and Eddie coming. One of the kids stopped. The other kid bumped into him, fell off his bicycle directly into the path of the oncoming skateboards, and began to cry.

Eddie stomped on the tail of his board and ground to a board-crunching halt. As he stopped, he reached out and gave Vickie a tremendous shove. She jerked forward and tore loose from the hedge and shot back across the sidewalk.

The kid's mouth was open. Vickie was so close, she could see the gap in his front teeth.

A parent began to shout.

I can't make it over the bikes, she thought. *But if I don't, I might kill a kid.*

There was no room between the bikes and the fire hydrant.

Eddie began to laugh.

Vickie thought, *If I make it, Skate'll never believe it.* She didn't have time to think about what would happen if she missed.

Arms flailing, heart pounding, Vickie launched her board into the air above the fire hydrant.

CHAPTER
3

She wasn't quite sure what happened next. One minute she was hanging in the air above the squat red hydrant while a babble of crying and angry shouting rose around her.

The next minute she had landed, unsteadily, on the street beyond the curb. She crouched instinctively as she landed, trying to keep her balance.

For a moment the world was a silent, perfect place. *I made it,* she thought.

"Spoiled-rotten kids!" an adult voice cried angrily.

" . . . tell your parents," another voice said. "There, there, baby, don't cry!"

Eddie had stopped laughing. But she heard him shout nastily. "Her name's Wheilson! *Vickie Wheilson,*" in the direction of the angry voices as he made his escape.

Vickie didn't look back. She still couldn't get her balance. The skateboard spun out of control, zigzagging crazily down the street. The shouting faded away behind her.

Desperately she grabbed at a parked car. Her hands slid off the door handle. She felt her wrist guards scrape the car door. At the last moment her fingers caught the side mirror.

Her board shot out from under her and across the street. The mirror turned upward and broke off in her hand.

She fell on her back on the road.

"Ugh," she said.

"You fell!" said a delighted voice. "You got in trouble!"

Vickie sat up and glared. Skate was standing there, holding his five-year-old sister, Christine's, hand.

"I made the fire hydrant," said Vickie. She pushed her bangs off her forehead. "It was a close call, this close, I swear, and I made it. It was awesome."

Skate rolled his eyes.

"Hey! I *did*! It would have been perfect, too, if it hadn't been for Eddie Hoover. He started the whole thing! Did you see that?"

Skate nodded.

Christine tugged on his hand, pulling him across the street. She bent and picked up one end of Vickie's board. She dragged it back across the street, letting the nose drag with a noise that made Vickie wince.

"Thanks, Chrissie," she said quickly, taking the board out of the kid's hand. She got up.

"I hate Eddie. He's a show-off. A hot dog. A big zero-talent meathead!"

Skate nodded again.

"I could beat him with one foot tied behind my back. I could beat him blindfolded!"

Skate gave Vickie a look. He liked Vickie. But she often boasted about things she couldn't do. Like now.

On the other hand sometimes she wasn't just bragging.

"Someone needs to teach that incredible hulk a lesson," Vickie fumed.

"Is your skateboard broken?" asked Christine, pointing.

"No!" shouted Vickie.

Christine stuck her lip out in a pout.

Vickie ignored Christine. She ignored the disapproving look Skate gave her. She had other things to think about. She thought deeply all the way up Skate's driveway. She thought deeply as she propped her skateboard next to his inside the back door. She thought deeply as she and Chrissie and Skate sat down at the kitchen table to drink Flightjuice (the choice of skateboard champions).

At last she said, ominously, "Someday, Eddie Hoover's going to get it good. And you know what, I'm going to laugh when it happens."

Skate said, "You jumped the hydrant."

Vickie looked at Skate. Skate looked at Vickie.

She grinned and took a big drink of Flightjuice. "Hah!" she said. "You told me I wasn't ready."

Skate rolled his eyes. But he grinned back. Then he said, "I'll be glad when Eddie gets it too."

"Jerk alert," muttered Vickie to herself.

Eddie Hoover was standing on the edge of one of the steps leading up to Graveyard School with Roy. As Vickie walked toward him, Eddie threw out his hands. He waved them in big circles and stood on one foot, pretending to barely be able to keep his balance.

"Oooh, look at mee!" he cried in a high voice. "I can jump fire hydrants on my skateboard!"

People turned to stare, and Vickie felt herself blushing. "Hey, Eddie," she said. "You *are* a fire hydrant. That's why dogs are always following you around."

Eddie's little mean eyes got littler and meaner. "Oh, yeah?"

"Yeah," said Vickie, "And *you* couldn't have made it over that fire hydrant anyway."

"Oh, yeah?" repeated Eddie.

"Careful, Eddie. You're gonna use up all your vocabulary words." Vickie kept going.

Good one, she thought. *Now he's going to kill me.*

But just then Maria Medina, who was standing with Polly and Stacey Carter at the top of the stairs, raised her hand and waved. Vickie waved back and took the steps two at a time until she reached them.

"So tell us all about it," said Maria.

Vickie was surprised. How had Maria heard about the fire-hydrant jump? She knew they hadn't been talking to Eddie. And she didn't think they'd been talking to Skate.

"It was nothing," she told Maria and the others modestly.

"Nothing!" exclaimed Maria. "No one's ever done it before!"

"Sure they have," said Vickie. "Skate can do it."

"Since when can Skate make it down Dead Man's Curve alive?" Polly said scornfully.

"Dead Man's Curve? What are you talking about?" asked Vickie.

Now Maria looked surprised. "The guy who's been going down Dead Man's Curve. What else? Although," she added thoughtfully, "it might not be a guy. No one's seen who it is up close."

"What guy? What are you *talking* about?" Vickie nearly screamed.

Stacey tossed her long braid over her shoulder. "What are you shouting for?" she asked.

"I'm not shouting!"

"Someone's been going down Dead Man's Curve," interrupted Polly. She smoothed her skirt carefully. The skirt was pink to match her pink-and-white-striped shirt, her pink tights, and the big pink-and-white bow that held her blond hair back today. "So I guess Skate won't be the first anymore. Or you."

Vickie couldn't help but look down at her own clothes. She was wearing pink too. Neon-pink sneakers. But like Maria and Stacey and everyone except Polly, she was wearing jeans. Maria was wearing one of her older brother's enormous rugby shirts over a dark-green turtleneck sweater. Stacey was wearing a denim shirt and a denim jacket. Vickie was wearing a sweatershirt with a hood, and her favorite baseball cap.

Vickie decided that Polly did not look pretty in pink. Ignoring her and her nasty, satisfied expression, Vickie said, "When did this happen? Who saw it?"

"Yesterday afternoon. Some third-grade soccer players saw it after practice while they were waiting for their ride. It wasn't you or Skate, was it?"

Thinking hard, Vickie shook her head. Yesterday afternoon she'd been trying not to die in a close encounter of the skateboard kind with disgusting Eddie Hoover. Yesterday afternoon Skate had been trapped at home baby-sitting.

"Has anyone told Skate? He's gonna hate this," said Vickie.

Polly smirked.

"I know," said Maria sympathetically.

"No one's seen Skate yet this morning," said Stacey. The others nodded.

"I can't believe this. Was the guy good? What happened?"

"That's all I know," said Maria.

Just then Polly said, "There's Skate."

Vickie turned quickly. She started down the stairs toward Skate. But Eddie had been waiting for Skate too.

As Skate swooped up to the front steps, he flipped his board up and into his hands all in one quick, casual motion. When Eddie did that, it looked like hard work. No wonder Eddie hated Skate, thought Vickie. *And no wonder I hate Eddie,* she thought as Eddie called Skate's name.

"Hey, Skate!" Eddie said, his voice dripping with phony friendliness. "Good work!"

Skate looked up, puzzled.

"I hear you made it down Dead Man's Curve yesterday afternoon."

Frowning, Skate shook his head.

"Skate," said Vickie, reaching the bottom of the stairs breathlessly. "I've got to tell you something!"

Skate held up his hand for Vickie to wait. He kept staring up at Eddie.

"Yep," said Eddie. "We heard all about it, didn't we, Roy?"

Roy gave a jackallike yelp of laughter.

"They said you just sort of disappeared after you finished your run. So I wanted to be the first to congratulate you," Eddie said.

Vickie was close enough to see Skate's face grow pale. But all he said was, "Yeah?"

"That *was* you, wasn't it?" asked Eddie, a big, mean grin on his face.

"Nope," said Skate.

"Gee, I'm *so* sorry," said Eddie. "I must have made a mistake. I should've known that *you* would never be able to make it down Dead Man's Curve."

With that he burst out laughing. Roy and the others around Eddie did too.

The first bell rang. Still laughing, Eddie and his friends turned and swaggered into the school.

"Maybe it's not true," said Vickie. "I *hate* Eddie."

"That helps," said Skate. He wanted to be left alone.

He hated Eddie too. Worse, he hated whoever had beat him down Dead Man's Curve.

He'd never envied anyone for being better than he was. He knew he had a lot to learn.

But he would have given anything to be the first.

CHAPTER

4

"He's not coming," said Vickie. "Whoever he is."

Skate didn't answer. He crouched by his board, his arms wrapped around his knees, staring down the hill toward Dead Man's Curve.

Vickie sighed and flopped back on the grass. "The sun has gone down, Skate," she said. "There are stars in the sky. It's getting late."

"Mmm," said Skate.

"Well, I'm cold. And hungry."

Something swooped out of the trees overhead. Vickie squinted up and added, "And now the bats are starting to come out.

"You know, Skate, maybe it wasn't a real person everybody saw up here. I was thinking, remember when we were up here and we heard something?" Vickie lowered her voice dramatically.

"What if it's a ghost?"

Skate shook his head. Vickie's mind worked in weird ways. Here he was, waiting to meet a champion skateboarder, a true vert dog, the one who had come out of nowhere to spin Dead Man's Curve—and she was talking about ghosts.

Sometimes, listening to Vickie, it was hard to believe he and Vickie were cousins. Hard to believe they came from the same family.

"It could be," Vickie insisted. "You know what some people say—Dead Man's Curve got its name because some kid on a skateboard refused to bail . . . Boom! Wipeout. Permanently. Know what I mean?"

"Nah," said Skate. But he did know what she meant. He'd thought about it himself. He just didn't want to tell her he had.

Maybe they were from the same family after all.

Vickie went on, "So the kid comes back, see? We've done something to annoy his ghost, or maybe he can't rest, and he comes back and he lures us up here and . . . eeeek! What're you doing? Did you see something?"

Skate had jumped up. He picked up his board. It was time to go.

"Oh." Relieved, Vickie got up too. "Maybe he's buried in that grave down there that everyone says glows in the dark." She nodded in the direction of the graveyard.

"No, it's some high school flight master," said Skate. "Or"—he turned toward Vickie, unable to conceal his enthusiasm— "a famous boardman. He's here to practice in *secret*." When he thought about it that way, it didn't hurt so much that someone else had beat him down Dead Man's Curve. In fact it didn't bother him at all.

"Yeah, right," Vickie answered sarcastically. She stopped. "Wait! Do you hear that?"

They'd just reached the boulders. From beyond came a faint *scritch-scritch*ing, like a wheel on a skateboard slightly out of sync.

"Maybe that's him!" gasped Vickie. "Let's go!"

Eager to be the first to see the mysterious skateboarder, she ran ahead of Skate into the dark on the other side of the rocks.

And began to scream.

She half jumped, half fell back up the road, scrambling toward Skate, her eyes so wide, Skate could see the whites all around them.

"It's him. The ghost! It's himmmmm!" she screamed.

Something white leaped out after Vickie.

Skate almost dropped his board, He couldn't believe his eyes.

The thing grabbed her by the ankle.

Vickie kicked wildly. "No, no, no!" she screamed.

Managing to keep a tight grip on his board, Skate leaped forward and grabbed Vickie's arm with his free hand to pull her loose.

Then he realized that the ghost was laughing.

Another ghost came out to join the first one. It was laughing too.

The first ghost pulled off its white covering. So did the second ghost.

Eddie Hoover and Roy Carne stood in front of Skate and Vickie, laughing themselves sick.

"It's the ghost! It's the ghost!" said Eddie in a high voice, mimicking Vickie.

"Ooh, don't hurt me!" added Roy.

Vickie scrambled to her feet. Skate pretended to examine his board.

He should have known Eddie would do something like that.

"Drop dead!" screamed Vickie, She shoved Eddie to one side and stormed down the Curve.

Skate followed her. For once Vickie had nothing to say as they walked past the graveyard and into the old parking lot, Above them they heard Eddie and Roy laughing until they reached the road.

Vickie still didn't feel like talking at school the next day. She got there late to avoid Eddie and Roy.

She met Dr. Morthouse in the hall and got marked for tardiness.

She spent the rest of the day slumped in her seat, her arms folded, brooding.

"It's over," Skate offered.

"Thanks for telling me," snapped Vickie. "Now tell Eddie."

Eddie spent the whole day saying in a high voice, every time he saw Vickie, "It's the ghost! It's the ghost!"

"Eddie's a creep," Maria Medina told Vickie at lunch. "He'll get his someday."

"Someday's not soon enough," said Vickie, glaring across the lunchroom at the table where Eddie and his friends were sitting.

"You don't really believe in ghosts, do you?" asked Polly. "That's for little kids."

"Polly," said Vickie, leaning over and making herself look as mean as possible. "Shut up!"

Polly's face got red. She looked down at her lunch and said, "I can say whatever I want." But she didn't say anything else.

Vickie made Skate leave the Hill that afternoon before the sun went down.

"It's giving me the creeps up here," she complained as they walked down the hill. When they reached the boulders, she marched between them, her chin up.

Nothing.

They went over the bridge, their feet echoing hollowly on the old planks. Skate stopped and leaned over to stare down into the deep, narrow channel that lay several feet below. A chilly mist was curling up off the water. Curls of spray shot over the rocks as the dark, cold water rushed beneath them and down the hill.

"Are you stalling?" demanded Vickie. "You are, aren't you? Can we go now?"

"You don't really believe in ghosts, do you?" asked Skate, turning with one last, reluctant look up the hill.

Vickie narrowed her eyes at her cousin. "You know what?" she said. "You talk too much!"

CHAPTER
5

School was out. The road was smooth. The light was good.

The day stunk.

Eddie Hoover and Roy Carne were boarding Skateboard Hill.

Skate stopped at the bottom and stared up. He couldn't believe his eyes. Eddie was a show-off, a trick stealer.

And a faker. At least that's what Skate had always thought.

But now Eddie was practicing his moves on Skateboard Hill. And, Skate had to admit, he wasn't as bad as Skate had thought he would be.

Then Skate got a better look at the board Eddie was riding.

"Awesome," he said, in spite of himself. He was glad no one was around to hear him.

It was a monster board—with a monster price. Skate knew because he'd seen it at the mall in the display window that summer, right before he'd broken his collarbone. He'd even gotten the sales guy to take it out; a long, sleek midnight-blue board with flecks of silver in it that glinted in the light like diamonds.

"Graphite core," the clerk had explained, "with a high-flex, guaranteed crack- and chip-proof veneer. Totally new engineering breakthroughs in balance and torque. And check out the wheels."

Skate had put the board down reverently in the aisle of the store and taken a tentative ride. It had been short and sweet. The board had felt as if it was molded to his foot. And as if at any moment it might take flight like a magic carpet.

"We didn't get but one of these," the clerk had said, taking the board and putting it back into the display window. "They only made a few, as a sort of test. And of course a top-of-the line piece of equipment like this—it costs."

The clerk pointed to the price tag propped in the window next to the board. Skate hadn't noticed it before.

His mouth dropped. His heart dropped farther.

The board could never be his. Not in a hundred allowances and summer jobs. He'd be driving a car before he could buy a board like that.

With one last, longing look at the board Skate had

turned away. He'd never looked in the window again. But he knew the board was there. He could feel it as he walked by, calling his name.

It almost made him feel disloyal to his own board.

The sight of Eddie on the board made him feel sick.

Skate was about to turn and go when Eddie saw him. "Hey, McGraw! You're not going, are you?"

Reluctantly Skate began the long walk up Dead Man's Curve. He didn't like to hate people. Unlike Vickie, he didn't spend time thinking about ways to get even with Eddie. He didn't think of Eddie at all. Eddie was just one of the people who gave skateboarding a bad name. Nothing more.

Until now.

Now Skate hated Eddie.

He reached the top of the hill and put down his board.

"What do you call that board?" said Eddie. "The dinosaur?"

Stupid Roy Carne cracked up, as if Eddie were the funniest guy in the world.

Without answering, Skate checked his gear. Everything secure. But before he could take off, Eddie said, "I guess you're blind, McGraw. Or maybe you don't know a decent skateboard when you see one." Eddie thumped his foot against the board resting at his feet for emphasis.

Not quite looking at Eddie or the board, Skate mumbled, "New."

"Guess you didn't notice it at the gear shop at the mall," said Eddie, "That's funny. I thought I saw you in there one day giving it a ride."

Skate shrugged. Then he forced himself to say, "Nice."

"How would you know?" asked Eddie.

"Yeah," said Roy. "How would you know?"

Far below, Skate saw Vickie charging up the hill, her gear on, her board under her arm. If things were bad now, they were about to get worse. Vickie knew how Skate felt about that board.

"Maybe you'd like a ride," said Eddie. "Just to see what a real board feels like." He pushed the nose of the board toward Skate temptingly. It bumped the rail guard on Skate's board gently.

For a moment Skate thought he felt his own board recoil in disgust.

But of course that wasn't possible.

Vickie had arrived. She saw the board immediately. "Where'dja get that piece of junk, Hoover?" she asked.

"I'd offer you a ride," Eddie said, "but I'm afraid you might fall over a fire hydrant."

Eddie and Roy started laughing even more loudly. Vickie's face turned red.

Eddie went on. "I offered McGraw here a ride, but he's afraid."

"Skate's not afraid," Vickie almost shouted, feeling her face turn even redder. She looked at Skate.

"Oh, yeah?" asked Roy. "Then how come he can't even make it down Dead Man's Curve?"

"No one's made it down Dead Man's Curve. I don't see *you* doing it," Vickie answered.

Roy smiled a nasty smile at Vickie. "Maybe I could, maybe I couldn't. But Eddie could. Couldn't you, Eddie?"

The new board had given Eddie a new confidence. "No problem," he said. "But then, maybe if you got a *real* board, McGraw, you could make it too."

"My board's as good as yours any day," Skate heard himself saying. "I could beat you on my board with one foot tied behind my back."

Vickie's mouth dropped open. Even Eddie and Roy seemed surprised by Skate's sudden ferociousness. But not as surprised as Skate was himself. Where had that come from? he wondered.

He didn't have time to think about it. Eddie smiled so hugely that all his big, ugly teeth showed like a row of tiles in a bathroom. He said, "You think so, McGraw? I don't. My board could beat your board anywhere, anytime."

Before Skate could answer, Vickie had put both

hands on her hips, "Oh, yeah, Hooverhead?" she said. "Well, Skate'll be the first person down Dead Man's Curve. On his board. A *real* board."

Eddie leaned over until he and Vickie were almost nose to nose. "How about a little match? Me on my board against McGraw on his, Down Dead Man's Curve. Winner gets both boards."

A long silence fell. Vickie looked at Skate. Eddie looked at Skate. Roy looked at Skate.

Skate looked down at his board. What would he do if he lost his board? He'd never have another like it. Suddenly he wished he'd never seen Eddie's board, never wanted it. Eddie's board was going to ruin his life.

He looked from his board to Eddie's. It sat there beneath Eddie's big, dumb, clumsy foot. The best board in the world couldn't make Eddie a better boarder. And Skate knew he was better than Eddie.

He looked up into Eddie's little shark eyes. "Now?" he asked.

That stopped Eddie. He hadn't been expecting it. His gaze dropped to his own board. It shifted to Dead Man's Curve.

For a moment Skate thought he'd bluffed Eddie out. Then, with an inward groan, he heard Vickie say, "What's the matter, Eddie? Chicken?"

For a moment Skate not only hated Eddie—he wanted to kill his cousin.

Eddie said, "I'm not chicken. But . . . but let's make this really interesting. Why don't we do the hill at night? At midnight?"

"In the dark?" scoffed Vickie.

"No. In the full moon." Eddie paused for effect, then said, "And the next full moon is Halloween."

Vickie opened her mouth.

Skate jumped in. "Fine."

Vickie's mouth dropped open farther.

Eddie and Roy began to laugh. Eddie pushed off and Roy followed him. They swooped down the hill. Eddie's new board caught fire in the sun, glittering, glinting. They hung a right onto Skateboard Hill. As they disappeared from sight, Eddie shouted, "See you then. Suckerrrrrrr."

"Boy is Eddie gonna be sorry," said Vickie. "You're going to take him *out,* Skate. I mean, take him totally *out.* He's gonna be road hamburger. Wheel meat. He'll be doing a Mr. Wilson all the way home."

Skate looked at his cousin. "Vickie."

"What?"

"You talk too much."

To his surprise Vickie nodded. Then she said, with false friendliness, "So, you don't think you can do it? You don't think you can beat that jerk Eddie Hoover?"

She tried not to let Skate see how anxious she was to hear his answer. How much she wanted him to say, "No problem."

She didn't let him see how worried she suddenly was when he didn't.

Instead Skate said, "I could beat Hoover. But I don't know if I can do Dead Man's Curve."

"Practice," began Vickie eagerly.

Skate shook his head. He looked up the hill. He looked down the hill. "I need to find that guy," he said at last. "The one who can do Dead Man's Curve."

"Then we will," said Vickie confidently.

But she said it with more confidence than she felt. She knew it and Skate knew it.

They practiced the rest of the afternoon. But for once Skate talked more than Vickie.

Because Vickie didn't talk at all.

CHAPTER

6

"Is it true?" asked Maria, coming up beside Vickie. Vickie had just made her escape from her mom and her older sister, who were shopping for dresses at the other end of the mall. She had to be back in half an hour. Now Vickie was standing in front of the window of the sports store staring at the display inside.

The theme was wheels: skates, bicycles, in-line skates, and skateboards. Vickie barely noticed the incredible bicycle suspended by wires from the ceiling of the display. The in-line skates left her cold. She was brooding over the hole in the display. No one had put another skateboard in the place of the one Eddie had bought. But then no other skateboard could match Eddie's new board.

Except maybe Skate's own board.

"Yeah," said Vickie listlessly, turning to face Maria

and Stacey. They were both holding sodas, and Maria had a huge shopping bag. "Yeah, it's true. Eddie bought the skateboard."

"What skateboard?" asked Stacey.

"Silly," Maria said to Vickie. "Is it true that Eddie and Skate are going to have a *duel*? On their skateboards?"

"Everybody's talking about it," Stacey added matter-of-factly.

Vickie was shocked. She ran her hands through her short hair until it was sticking up all over her head even more. "They are? But it just happened!"

Maria snorted. "Eddie has a big mouth."

"He's got a big head too. Skate'll beat him, easy." Stacey took a long slurp of the soda she was holding and offered it to Vickie.

"Thanks," said Vickie. She took a slurp too. She felt slightly better because of Stacey's words. "You really think Skate can beat Eddie?"

"Eddie's a hot dog. A show-off. Skate'll kill him," Stacey said.

Maria nodded. "Eddie," she said, her dark eyes disgusted. "He deserves whatever happens to him. I'm gonna laugh when Skate wipes Eddie out."

Vickie wished she had Maria's and Stacey's confidence. But she had seen Skate trying to make it down Dead Man's Curve. He hadn't looked like someone who could make it.

Maybe a coach *was* just what he needed. A little help couldn't hurt after all.

Trying to sound casual, she said, "Hey, have you guys heard anything more about the skateboarder that people saw going down Dead Man's Curve the other day?"

Stacey shook her head. Maria twisted one dark strand of hair around her finger thoughtfully. She said, "It was some third-grader that saw it. She's . . . I think someone said she's the goalie on one of the junior soccer teams. You could ask her."

"You gonna try to find the guy?" asked Stacey. "Why?"

"Maybe," said Vickie. She changed the subject before Stacey could ask any more questions. "What did you guys buy?"

"A new rugby shirt," said Maria happily. She reached in the bag and pulled out a long-sleeved blue shirt with a white collar and a yellow stripe across it.

"Maria, you've got a thousand rugby shirts," said Vickie. "More than anyone else in the world."

"Well, now I have a thousand and one," said Maria, grinning. "You can't have too many rugby shirts."

"You can. You do," said Stacey.

The three of them walked back down the mall. Stacey and Maria kept arguing about rugby shirts. Vickie nodded every once in a while to show she was listening.

But she wasn't. She was thinking about the duel on Dead Man's Curve. It had seemed like such a great idea at first: she'd been so sure that Skate could beat Eddie. And when he did, Eddie would not only lose his board but he'd look stupider than ever.

It was the perfect revenge.

She hadn't stopped to think what would happen if Eddie didn't lose. She didn't like to think about it now. Because if Eddie won and Skate lost, it would be all her fault.

Skate needed all the help he could get.

She had to find the mystery skateboarder before it was too late. It was the least she could do.

The third-grader jumped like a scared rabbit when Vickie grabbed her by the arm.

"You were the one who saw the guy on Dead Man's Curve?" demanded Vickie.

The kid drew herself up to her full height. She cleared her throat. She nodded.

Vickie rolled her eyes. Great. If the kid talked the way Skate talked, they would be there all day.

"And?" said Vickie, trying to make her voice encouraging and menacing at the same time.

The kid cleared her throat again and said in a rush, "Last week. After soccer practice. It wasn't just me. We were waiting for our ride. Coach was there too."

"Did you see who it was?"

The kid stopped talking again. She shook her head.

"What was he—or she—wearing?"

Another shake of the head.

Vickie gritted her teeth.

The kid said, "Skinny. It was a real skinny person."

"Now we're getting somewhere," said Vickie. "Old? Young? Long hair? Short hair? Male? Female? Dark hair? Light hair? Dark skin? Light skin?"

The kid stopped talking again and shook her head.

With a sigh Vickie said, "But you're sure you saw this person go all the way down Dead Man's Curve?"

A nod.

"Standing up?"

Another nod.

"Without falling and without stopping?"

The kid nodded vigorously. Then she said, "It was awesome."

"When was it? When did this happen?"

"After soccer practice. I told you . . . ."

"What day?" said Vickie. She wanted to scream, but she made her voice stay calm.

Ducking her head, the kid thought deeply. At last she said, "Wednesday. Practice was over. We were all leaving."

"Other people saw this thrasher besides you?"

The kid looked puzzled.

"The guy on the skateboard, Other people were with you and they saw him—or her—too?"

"Oh. Yeah. Carmelita and Phillip and—"

" Thanks." Vickie let go of the kid's arm, giving up.

Faster than a speeding soccer ball, the kid took off down the hall and out of Vickie's reach.

Standing there with her hands on her hips, her spikey red hair sticking up everywhere, in her purple sweatshirt and ripped jeans and crash-tested-to-the-max orange high-tops, Vickie shook her head. What was the kid scared of?

Little kids were so weird.

Oh, well, she thought. It wasn't much to go on, but it was better than nothing. The mystery skateboarder had been seen by plenty of witnesses. At least he was real.

"This is the *last* time, Skate," said Vickie.

Skate made a face. Vickie had been complaining all afternoon. A wheel felt loose. Her helmet was too tight. The road was too bumpy. The sun was too bright.

Now she was saying it was too late. "I don't like it up here in the dark. That guy's not gonna show up this late. What's the point? He'd be running the hill blind. It would be insane. Inhuman—"

Cutting Vickie off by putting his foot on his board, Skate nodded slightly. He motioned for Vickie to go ahead. Hotdogging, she jumped on her board with both feet and shot off the top of Skateboard Hill.

Skate pushed off behind her.

He hadn't gone far before he realized that someone was coming up behind him.

Eddie, thought Skate disgustedly. He pulled himself in and prepared for a sideswipe or some snakelike shredding maneuver.

Then he realized that it wasn't Eddie. It wasn't anybody he recognized.

It was a tall, skinny guy dressed in faded jeans and an enormous, patched denim shirt that flapped in the wind. His funky old boots were planted on a gleaming jet-black board with a row of extremely realistic flames painted on the sides.

Skate saw it all in a glance.

And realized immediately that it was the mystery thrasher.

Instinctively he dropped one foot off the board and dragged to a stop.

The guy powered to a stop in a stand-up slide.

Skate's mouth dropped open. It was *not* a stopping technique he would have been able to use on a hill as steep as this part of Skateboard Hill.

Down below, swinging to the right to avoid Dead Man's Curve, Vickie looked back. She saw the thrasher too. Her stop was the least elegant of all. She swerved into the grass and tumbled off.

Skate didn't see Vickie's landing. He was staring at

the mirror image of himself reflected back in the mystery boarder's midnight-black shades.

"It's you," said Skate. "You're real!"

The guy smiled with thin lips. But the smile was gone as quickly as it had appeared. He stuck out a pale hand. "Ben Marrow," he said.

"Skate McGraw." Skate stuck out his own hand and shook the mystery skateboarder's. He winced at the bony pressure of Ben's cold fingers. But then he forgot about it as he realized what was oddest of all about Ben Marrow.

The guy was skateboarding equipment-free. He didn't have a helmet on his head—just long, sort of colorless hair pulled back into a ponytail. He wasn't wearing knee pads or elbow pads or even wrist braces. Skate couldn't believe it. Hamburgering himself to doom in a major skateboard bail was not Skate's idea of the way to go. Painful. Messy.

Skate wanted to die riding his skateboard, sure. Someday. But he wanted to go clean.

A person had to be incredibly confident or incredibly stupid to go without even wearing wrist guards. Or maybe both.

Skate's heart sank. Maybe this Marrow guy was a suicide rider. Maybe *that* was the only way to take Dead Man's Curve.

"Nice deck," said Marrow in a low, scratchy voice, nodding his head at Skate's board.

Skate looked down. "Thanks. Yours too."

"Out of this world," said Marrow. "But it's not everybody's ride, y'know?" He smiled again.

Vickie was pumping up the hill toward them. Skate said quickly, "You can do Dead Man's Curve."

"It's a nice curve," answered Marrow as if the Curve were nothing more than a long, gradual turn down an easy bank.

Skate gulped. "I can't. Make it down the Curve, I mean."

Even though he couldn't see Marrow's eyes, Skate sensed his surprise. Or was it amusement? It was hard to tell anything about the guy behind the enormous shades he was wearing, Skate wondered how he could see. It was nearly dark.

But that wasn't important. Skate said, even more quickly, "So I was wondering, since you can do the Curve, maybe you could give me some ideas. On how to do it, you know?"

"You mean how to beat Eddie Hoover," interrupted Vickie, pushing up between them. "You're the guy, aren't you? The one all the little kids saw going down Dead Man's Curve."

"Did they?" asked Marrow. "All the, er, little kids? How unusual."

"I'm Vickie."

"Ben Marrow," said the guy, extending his hand a second time to shake Vickie's.

53

She gave it a quick pump, not seeming to notice its bony coldness. "Awesome board," she said. "Excellent. Listen, Mr. Marrow—"

"Call me Ben," Marrow said smoothly.

"Ben, we need your help. Eddie-the-Snake Hoover has challenged Skate to a duel, see? Skate's better, but Eddie has this incredible new board. Eddie's got more money than brains, but then if you've got twenty-five cents you've more money than Eddie's got brains. Anyway—"

Skate couldn't stand it anymore. He interrupted his cousin. "Hoover gets my board if he wins. I get his if I win. The ride is Dead Man's Curve," said Skate.

Marrow turned his head slightly toward the Curve. The sun had gone down, and the fiery flames of the sunset skyline danced across the shining-dark lenses of his glasses.

"Will you do it?" asked Vickie. "Will you tell Skate how to make it down Dead Man's Curve?"

Marrow turned back to face Skate and Vickie. He smiled. "I believe we could work out a deal," he said.

"Excellent," said Vickie.

"What kind of a deal?" asked Skate.

"You like your board?" Marrow pointed at Skate's board.

"Yeah. And it's not part of any deal."

"Seems to me it already is," said Marrow. "Isn't that what you just told me'?"

Skate opened his mouth. He closed it again. The guy had a point.

Marrow stroked his pointed chin. "Ah. Well, what's one skateboard more or less? If you lose, you lose it anyway."

"Yeah, but what's the point of winning if he has to give *you* his board?" argued Vickie. "He might as well just try to make it on his own. That way if he wins, he keeps his board."

"True," said Marrow. His voice had a raspy sound, as if he wasn't used to talking much.

Do I sound like that when I talk? wondered Skate.

Marrow smiled again.

Vickie frowned suddenly.

"Hmmm," said Marrow. "A skateboared for a skateboard . . . hardly my idea of a high-stakes prize anyway. Paltry. Unimaginative in fact."

"Hey, Skate's board is *the* best. Including Eddie's," said Vickie hotly, frowning more than ever.

The dark glasses turned toward Vickie, then back toward Skate. "I'm sure we could work out something with a little more style, a little more imagination, Skate McGraw. My lessons for . . . what? What's it worth to you?"

"I don't know . . ." said Skate.

"*Come on*, Skate," Vickie said.

Marrow raised an eyebrow. His eyebrows were the same pale color as his hair.

"Well, uh . . ." Skate began.

"My services guarantee you'll win," said Marrow. "What is that worth to you?"

"All I have is my skateboard," said Skate.

Marrow shook his head. "You disappoint me, Skate McGraw," he said. "Think about it. We'll talk again."

"When?" demanded Vickie.

Marrow said, "Tomorrow. Perhaps."

Then he was gone. In a whoosh of cold air at an impossible speed he disappeared without a sound into the darkness between the boulders at the entrance to Dead Man's Curve.

CHAPTER

7

The cold made the hair on Vickie's neck stand up. She realized that she was clutching her board against her like a shield and she loosened her grip.

"What a weirdo," said Vickie. Suddenly she wasn't so certain that Marrow was the man to coach Skate to victory over Eddie Hoover and Dead Man's Curve.

But Vickie's uncertainty seemed to reassure Skate. He shrugged and dropped his board on the ground. Slowly, side by side, they headed down Skateboard Hill for home.

At the corner of Vickie's street they stopped. The streetlights were just coming on. Vickie shivered. "It's getting cold," she said. "Almost as cold as up on Skateboard Hill."

"Hills are colder," said Skate.

"That Marrow guy's weird," said Vickie. "You know what I think?"

Skate shrugged. She'd tell him anyway.

Vickie said, "I think you did the right thing, to pull a stall on him. I think you don't need him maybe, after all."

"He's good," said Skate.

"Weird," said Vickie.

"Excellent," said Skate. "Not good, excellent."

"Not just weird, *really* weird," said Vickie. "He gives me the creeps," she repeated, just for good measure.

Skate shrugged again, Then he, too, pushed off and disappeared into the shadows—although not as quickly or as silently as Ben Marrow.

Or as *weirdly,* thought Vickie.

But weird isn't bad, she argued with herself the rest of the way home. *So he's a little rude, a little strange. He's good. People probably think I'm weird. They probably think Skate's weird.*

Weird isn't bad. Weird is just weird.

It'll be okay, she concluded, kick-turning to a stop in her driveway. *I'm imagining things.*

Two days later Skate was still waiting to speak to Ben. Two days later he was up on Skateboard Hill, trying to break the curse of Dead Man's Curve.

And failing.

"One more time," he said to Vickie.

"Sure," she said cheerfully.

How could she be so cheerful at a time like this, Skate wondered.

Skate launched his board. He headed for Dead Man's Curve.

The graves along the road where it split came screaming toward him. Skate leaned. Forced himself to head for the Curve.

And lost his nerve.

If he'd had time, he would have broken out in a cold sweat of fear. But he was too busy bailing. He dropped his board into a tail grind and heard asphalt punishing wood, tearing it down. The wood sounded like it was crying in pain.

He couldn't do that to his board. He dropped back onto four wheels and did a dive onto the grass, rolling over and over. His board hit the grass on the far side, flipped, and landed wheels up.

Where was Ben Marrow when he needed him, thought Skate.

"Skate? Skaaaaate?"

"Fine," croaked Skate back to Vickie, who was standing at the top of the hill. After a moment he got up, snagged his board, and headed back up the road.

Vickie swooped by and angled down Skateboard Hill away from the entrance to the Curve. She waved at Skate as she went by.

Skate scowled.

How could she be in such a good mood when Ben Marrow hadn't bothered to show up? When the days to Halloween were slipping away?

When he was in danger of losing his board?

He was running out of time. Not only that, but every day of practice seemed to make him worse.

He wondered where Eddie was practicing. His parents had probably built him a full-scale model of Dead Man's Curve in his backyard, thought Skate bitterly. Eddie had probably hired special coaches.

You didn't see Eddie hanging out on Skateboard Hill in the cold and the dark.

Skate sighed and pushed off.

This time his wipeout was spectacular. His skateboard shot out from under him as if he were still a beginner. It spun around and around until it went off the road. Skate flipped up in the air and landed heavily on his back, knocking all the wind out of his chest.

Eddie was going to kill him. No question about it. If he didn't kill himself first.

A soft voice spoke almost in his ear. "Part of the trick is knowing how to fall, You *do* make it look hard."

Skate's eyes flew open. He sat up.

Ben Marrow was squatting on the road next to him.

"It's you," said Skate.

Marrow smiled, "In the flesh," he answered. His smile grew wider.

He had a lot of prominent teeth. It was hard to tell how old Marrow was. At first Skate had thought he was a high-schooler. But now he wasn't so sure.

Marrow didn't say anything. He just looked back at Skate, still smiling his wide, toothy smile.

Skate leaned over and peered past Marrow. Vickie had finished her run and was on her way back up the hill, head down, trudging slowly. But in a minute she would look up and see them. Skate had to cut his deal now, before Vickie got back.

"I need your help," said Skate. "I can't make it down the Curve. Eddie's gonna beat me and he's gonna get my board."

"A terrible thing," said Ben. He didn't sound as if he thought it was terrible at all.

That made Skate pause. What kind of skateboarder could be so casual about losing his board?

But Skate was desperate. He pushed the uneasy feeling aside.

"Maybe we could work something out," said Skate. "I can't give you my board, though. But . . . can you help me?"

"Yes. I can teach you everything I know about skateboarding. Everything. The education of a lifetime. No stone left unturned." The big white teeth flashed again.

"I can't give you my board," Skate repeated. His heart was pounding in his ears. His palms were beginning to sweat.

Ben nodded. He went on. "I guarantee you'll make

61

it down Dead Man's Curve. In fact you will make winning look easy. Dead easy. In exchange—"

"Hey!" Vickie had seen them. She was trotting now,
her head up as if she were a dog on the scent of a trail.

"What's the deal?" asked Skate hastily. "What do
you want?"

"What do I want? Not all that much. Just do exactly
as I tell you, and you will win. And in exchange you
will give me—"

"Hey!" said Vickie again, breathlessly. She broke
into a run and covered the last few yards between them
at top speed.

Skate made a face, trying to warn her off, but Ben
turned his head so quickly that Skate heard the bones
in Ben's neck crack. "Yes?" Ben said, sounding annoyed.

"What's going on?" asked Vickie, undisturbed by
the lack of welcome she was receiving.

Go away, Vickie, thought Skate. He cleared his
throat. He tried to catch her eye.

"We're talking about some skateboard lessons. Perhaps you would like some too."

"No thanks, Mr. Marrow—"

"Call me Ben."

"—and I don't think Skate needs them either."

Vickie had seen Skate try to catch her eye. She'd
heard him clear his throat. She didn't know what had
come over her.

But something about seeing Skate and Ben Marrow standing so close together at the top of Dead Man's Curve had made her blood run cold. No doubt about it, Ben Marrow wasn't wrapped right. In fact she was beginning to think he was beyond weird. Maybe all the way over into crazy.

Skate's mouth dropped open.

"Really?" said Ben.

"Vickie, get *lost,*" Skate hissed.

In answer Vickie grabbed her cousin's arm and pulled him off to one side. "Don't do it, Skate. You don't need this guy. There's something wrong with him!"

"Like what?"

"I don't know." Vickie lowered her voice. "But he's not the coach for you, Skate. Don't agree to let him coach you."

"You're just jealous. That's it, isn't it?" said Skate.

"Of what? He's good, okay. I'll give him that. But it's not enough, Skate. There's more to life—"

"Not for me there isn't," said Skate.

"Winning isn't everything, Skate."

"Oh yeah? So if I lose my skateboard, that's okay too? Maybe that's what you wanted all along, Vickie. Maybe it's the only way you know how to beat me at skateboarding."

Vickie's face turned as red as her jacket.

Skate yanked his arm free from Vickie's grip and

turned back toward Ben Marrow. "Deal," he said as he turned.

But he was too late.

Ben Marrow was gone.

"Ben?" said Skate. "Ben Marrow?"

His words hung mockingly in the near darkness.

"He's gone," said Vickie.

"Duh," Skate answered. He felt a surge of anger make his feet hot.

Emotions always affected him in his feet first.

"Ben!" he shouted. "Come back! You've got a deal!"

But no one answered.

Anger raced through him so strongly, he thought his feet had caught on fire. "Thanks a lot!" he yelled, turning back to Vickie.

Vickie's eyes widened. She took a little step back. "W-what?"

"I'm going to lose my board. Eddie Hoover's going to beat me and make me look like a dwid. And it's because of you!" shouted Skate.

Hearing Skate admit—in so many words—that Eddie might be able to beat him made Vickie want to gag. It also made her angry. How could Skate talk like that? "How can you talk like that!" Vickie heard her voice going up. She took a deep breath and tried to calm down. "You'll *destroy* Eddie. Erase him. Make him into skid marks! You don't need anybody's help! You just need practice."

"I *am* practicing. I'm nearly perfect at wipeouts now, in case you haven't noticed. Thanks for all your help, Vickie. What did Eddie do, pay you to set me up?"

Vickie felt as if someone had punched her in the stomach. Her face turned even redder.

Then she lost it. She leaned over and went nose to nose with Skate. "ME? ME??? That's right, blame me! When you lose to Eddie, blame me. Tell the whole world it's my fault that you can't do the Curve. Blame me, you . . . you . . . *loser!*"

Eyes blazing, hands on her hips, Vickie glared at her cousin, waiting for his answer.

But Skate didn't answer. He centered his board, dropped on, and pushed off in one swift, angry motion.

"Skate! Skate! Where are you going?" shouted Vickie in spite of herself.

Skate hung the words over his shoulder without slowing down. "To find Ben Marrow!"

CHAPTER

He was booking toward Dead Man's Curve. Going so fast, he could smell smoke coming off his wheels.

He was flying.

This time he was going to do it. No stopping. No turning back. No wiping out.

The wind rushed past, freezing cold.

A not-quite-full moon lit the way with frozen silver light. He crouched lower, lower, hanging on to his balance, hanging on to his speed.

Ahead the rocks of Dead Man's Curve loomed, glittering in the moonlight. To his left the tombstones were a blur.

The opening to the Curve had never seemed so narrow.

Something was wrong. Skate stole a quick look at

his board. But it was fine. Just the same. It would never let him down.

Then Skate looked back up.

And realized what he was looking at, The giant rocks on either side of the Curve's mouth had turned into gleaming teeth, the road was a red-black tongue, curling up beneath him.

He was skating into the jaws of death.

He tried to stop. Tried to swerve. Tried to bail any way he could.

But it was too late.

Too late even to scream.

But he screamed anyway. . . .

His little sister, Christine, stood at the door of his room, a tiny ghostly figure in a white nightgown, clutching a teddy bear.

Skate blinked. He looked around. He was sitting in his own bed in his own room. It had been a nightmare. Just a nightmare.

"Skate?" his little sister said again.

"Oh. Christine. Did I wake you up?"

Christine nodded solemnly.

"Sorry," said Skate. "Bad dream." Giving himself a mental shake, he got out of bed and took his little sister back to her room and tucked her in. She yawned hugely.

"Good night Skate," she said sleepily.

"No bad dreams now, okay?" he told her.

She nodded sleepily, her eyes already closing.

Lucky kid, thought Skate.

He went back to his room and lay down, his eyes wide open. Three days to go and he hadn't found Ben Marrow. No Marrows in the phone book. No one named Ben Marrow over at the high school. Where was he from? A college?

Had he gone back to school? The thought chilled Skate to the bones. He turned restlessly in the bed and groaned. The more he practiced, the more he fell. His knees were bruised even through the knee pads. His wrists ached from landing on the wrist guards to stop.

And he hadn't even made it past the two rocks that marked the entrance to the Curve. He slid to the left. He skidded to the right. The board slipped out from under him. His wheel caught on a rough spot in the road.

Something always went wrong.

And tomorrow he couldn't practice. He had to baby-sit his little sister. At last Skate closed his eyes. But he didn't sleep.

He didn't think he would ever sleep again.

Three days to Halloween and the excitement was running high at Graveyard School. Orange jack-o'-lantern cutouts decorated the windows of the classrooms. Teachers gave the usual lesson about the history of Halloween and included Halloween words on spelling tests and math problems.

Hannibal Lucre wandered the halls, smiling at the students, rubbing his hands together, and saying, "How are my little bats and goblins?"

Some of the first-graders laughed when he said this. Nervously.

Everyone talked about the duel between Eddie and Skate.

Vickie ignored them.

Skate ignored them.

Vickie ignored Skate.

Skate ignored Vickie.

Eddie never stopped talking.

In class he whispered as Skate walked by, "How do you spell 'Dead Man' McGraw?"

When the teacher gave them a creative-writing assignment, Eddie said loudly, "I'm gonna call mine, 'Dead Man on Dead Man's Curve.' Yeah. I like that."

At the top of his own paper Skate didn't write "Why the Olympics Need Skateboarding" or "How to Build the Perfect Skateboard." For the first time in his life he didn't feel like writing about skateboards at all.

He stared at the paper, He heard the snickers from Eddie and Eddie's friends. He *felt* Vickie ignoring him all the way across the room.

Eddie's right, thought Skate. I'm a dead man.

Slowly he wrote, "How I Spent My Summer Vacation."

The rocks loomed up.

Skate wiped out.

He heard his board flip and land wheels up. He listened to the wheels spin, then stop spinning.

He stared up at the sky. Dark blue. Getting darker.

Where was Eddie practicing, he wondered. And when?

He thought about running away from home.

He thought about Ben Marrow.

At last he stood up. Soon it would be dark and the Curve would be a suicide mission—at least until the moon came up.

He tried to imagine the Curve by moonlight.

It was the Curve of his nightmare.

Skate got up. He picked up his board and trudged back up the hill.

He tried the Curve again. He missed the Curve again.

It was too dark to go on now. Wearily Skate stood up. He didn't even feel like boarding Skateboard Hill on the way home.

He decided to walk down Dead Man's Curve.

I'll probably wipe out just walking, he thought bitterly. But if he didn't fall, walking it couldn't hurt. He could study the Curve.

As if he didn't know every inch of the Curve in his sleep.

His nightmares.

A test that never went away. A test he never passed and had to keep taking over and over and over again.

It was enough to make you hate skateboarding, Skate thought. And that was enough to ruin your life.

Skate picked up his board and started down the Curve. The moment he passed between the two boulders, the sun seemed to disappear altogether from the sky. Crossing the bridge, he leaned over to look down. Wisps of fog spun up off the water, twisting up into the darkness and disappearing. A draft of icy air rose up to brush with eerie coldness against his face.

Oooh, I'm scared, thought Skate sarcastically.

He looked back up the long, empty hill behind him. Where was Eddie practicing? Why wasn't Eddie worried about losing? Had Skate been kidding himself about being better on the board than Eddie?

Or was it just a big fake? A psych-out?

Nah. Eddie didn't have the brains for head games.

It was so dark now that his shoelaces looked clean and white on his sneakers. That definitely meant it was time to head home.

He started walking again. He was almost at the bottom of the hill when the figure rose up out of the graveyard and grabbed him by the arm.

CHAPTER

9

"AAAAAAAH!" Skate screamed. He swung his skateboard. "EEEEEEK!" Vickie screamed. She ducked.

"Vickie!" Skate shouted. "What are you *doing*?"

"You almost killed me!" Vickie looked at the board Skate was still holding over his head like a club. "Are you crazy?"

Skate couldn't believe it. "I'm not the one hiding in graveyards!"

"I wasn't hiding. I just got here and I saw you walking down and decided to wait," said Vickie. She was trying to breathe normally. She was trying to act as if Skate hadn't just scared her half to death.

Skate started walking again. "You could have warned me."

"I'm not speaking to you," Vickie said.

That stopped Skate. He turned to face Vickie.

"If you're not speaking to me, what're you doing here?"

"That's what I'm trying to tell you."

Folding his arms, Skate waited.

"Okay, okay. The thing is, I got you into this. You're right about that. So I thought I'd help you find Ben Marrow."

Skate kept his arms folded. He kept waiting.

Why was Skate being such a pain, wondered Vickie. "You're being a pain, you know that?" she said aloud.

Skate still didn't say anything.

So what else is new? thought Vickie. She gave up. "I give up," she said. "But I'm here to tell you that I don't think this Ben Marrow guy is normal, okay? Like he's not in the phone book, he's not from the high school, there's not even a family by that name listed in the whole town."

Skate said, "How did you know that?"

" 'Cause I checked."

"I did too."

Nodding, Vickie continued, "So where do you think this guy comes from, Skate?"

"He's a famous bizotic vert dog," said Skate. "He's gleaming new maneuvers and he's staying low."

"Yeah, right," scoffed Vickie. "He's bizarre and *maybe* exotic—but a famous skateboarder who's come all the way to our town just to practice a few tricks so nobody will steal them? I don't think so."

Skate didn't ask Vickie what she did think. He knew he didn't have to.

He was right. Vickie turned and pointed up the hill, "No, Skate. I'll tell you where Mr. Ben Marrow comes from. He comes from the old graveyard."

Skate's mouth dropped open. He looked in the direction Vickie's finger was pointing. The graves all gleamed the same dull white as his shoelaces. By the light of day they were all the same gray, dirty color.

But his shoelaces didn't make him nervous. The graveyard did. Especially when it got dark.

Like now.

"You're crazy," said Skate, making himself sound positive of the fact. He tore his gaze from the graveyard and looked back at Vickie. It was so dark, he could barely see her face. *I'm gonna get it for being late to dinner,* he thought.

"How did Dead Man's Curve get its name?" asked Vickie. "Someone died there, right?"

"No one's been buried there since the 1800s. And the earliest skateboards weren't until after that," Skate argued.

"It's doesn't have to be a skateboard that made the guy do a death bail. He's just choosing the best way to do some haunting."

"You *are* crazy," said Skate.

"Yeah? What're you? Chicken?"

Skate leaned forward until he could see the whites of his pain-in-the-board cousin's eyes. "No."

"Then let's go looking for Ben Marrow's grave."

"What makes you so sure?"

"Skate. He only comes out late. He's only been seen here. He doesn't have an address anywhere else. Know why? His address is written on one of those tombstones."

"Hah." Skate stared into Vickie's eyes.

"Hah?" Vickie stared right back. Finally Skate blinked.

Vickie smiled.

"Now?" said Skate.

"We're gonna get killed for getting home late anyway."

"Naw," said Skate, turning reluctantly to lead the way among the tombstones. "We're gonna get killed in the graveyard."

The moon was beginning to rise, fat and shadowy white, like a dirty dish. One edge of it looked ragged and broken.

Still two days until the full moon, thought Skate, watching his moon shadow slide over another grave. He squinted.

No one by the name of Ben Marrow there.

They'd started at the top of the graveyard and worked their way down. Vickie had brought a flashlight, but it was slow work. At first it had been scary work, walking across the uneven ground, trying not to stumble over broken headstones, feeling his sneakers sink ominously into the earth as if a grave was about to turn into quicksand beneath his feet.

But now it was just boring. And cold. He rubbed his nose, shifted his board to the other arm and bent over.

No Ben Marrow.

No one by that last name anywhere.

"Hey, maybe we missed it," he called nastily. "It was probably the glow-in-the-dark grave and we didn't see it."

"Maybe it is," answered Vickie, her flashlight bobbing along the last row of stones toward him. "Maybe it doesn't glow all the time, like people say. Maybe it only glows on special nights."

She came up beside Skate and switched the light off. She rubbed her eyes. "And maybe Ben Marrow isn't even his real name."

"It was a dumb idea," said Skate.

"Yeah?" Vickie was beginning to get annoyed again. This was the thanks she got for trying to help? "I don't see you coming up with a better idea."

"A stupid idea. Monster stupid."

"Kiss my skateboard!" answered Vickie, and turned to march away.

She stopped.

Skate bumped into her and stepped back.

A tall, skinny dark figure was lurching down the row of graves toward them.

"Ben?" Skate's voice came out thin and high.

No answer.

"Ben Marrow? Mr. Marrow?" croaked Vickie.

No answer.

"Who are y—"

The figure raised its long arms. It reached to grab them.

CHAPTER

10

Vickie crashed into Skate. Skate crashed into Vickie. They backed up and tried again.

Vickie fell. Skate fell over her.

Shoving Skate out of her way, Vickie scrambled to her feet. "It's not . . . it's . . . "

"BASEMENT BART!" shouted Skate.

They took off for home as fast as they could.

Mr. Bartholomew, janitor of Graveyard School, watched from the edge of the graveyard as the two figures disappeared at maximum speed into the night. He bared his teeth in a smile that would have made a dog growl and all but a very nearsighted person back up. He ran his tongue over his teeth.

"Next time," he muttered.

Then he turned and walked back across the parking lot, and through the door to the basement of Graveyard School.

• • •

"You're kidding," said Maria. She looked around as if he might hear her and lowered her voice. "Basement Bart? You got chased by Basement Bart?"

"You shouldn't have been in the graveyard." Polly Hannah shook her head primly.

"What *were* you doing in the graveyard?" asked Maria.

Vickie shrugged. She didn't think her idea had been a stupid one. But she couldn't prove it hadn't been either.

They hadn't found Ben Marrow.

"It's Halloween in two days," said Stacey. "Is Skate gonna win? Is he gonna make it down Dead Man's Curve?"

"Even if he doesn't, Eddie has to make the curve himself to win." Vickie said. "He won't." The thought gave her some comfort. Besides, she had to show her support of Skate, even if she wasn't speaking to him.

The four girls looked over at Eddie and his friends. "He can't," added Vickie.

Eddie and his friends were sitting at their usual table in the corner of the lunchroom, throwing food at the ceiling to see if it would stick, burping, making barf jokes, and seeing who could make the loudest gross noises. Vickie stared at Eddie.

Did he have nerves of steel? Or was he just too stupid to be nervous?

Or maybe he was nervous and trying to hide it. Taking a bite of her peanut butter sandwich and chewing thoughtfully, Vickie decided that Eddie looked a little— thinner? Paler? Not quite himself?

Think positive, she told herself. She closed her eyes and pictured Eddie wiping out into a full-body slam at the very top of Dead Man's Curve—and then going all the way to the bottom beneath the wheels of his own skateboard.

She felt better.

Skate walked slowly across the lunchroom. He didn't look to the right or to the left. He sat down at one of the unclaimed tables and began to eat. He stared out the window dully.

He was tired.

He'd lost the power to imagine ever making it down Dead Man's Curve standing up.

"Yo, Boardman! Skate. Boardmaster." Park Addams stopped at Skate's table.

Skate looked up and nodded.

"Just two days till Halloween. It is going to be an event. Major. A must-see. I'm wearing my kicking special Halloween costume, just for you."

Skate nodded again.

"Any special strategies? Like, new wheels? A new paint job? New bearings?"

Skate shook his head.

Park looked at Skate expectantly. Skate couldn't think of anything to say.

Finally Park said, "Yeah, why mess with success? Listen, don't worry. Practically the whole school is gonna be there. You're gonna be famous. You know?"

He gave Skate a thump on the back for emphasis and took off.

The whole school. Things couldn't get any worse. In fact, if the house burned down tonight and took his skateboard with it, things would only improve.

Only I couldn't run out of a burning house and leave my skateboard to fry, he thought. And he knew it was true.

He wiped out every time that afternoon, up on Dead Man's Curve. Not because his freedom and his allowance were in serious danger if he got home late for the second night in a row.

But because he was just too tired to go on.

Skate and Eddie met face-to-face on the school steps the day before Halloween.

"Haven't made it yet, have you?" Eddie asked Skate loudly.

Why do anything different? thought Skate. He shrugged and tried to walk past Eddie as if he didn't care.

Eddie slammed him with his shoulder.

Skate stepped back. "Save it for tomorrow night, Hoover."

"You're a chicken," said Eddie. "You don't deserve to win. That board is mine."

Was it possible? Skate wondered. Did his board actually flinch in the crook of his arm? He said, "I haven't seen you make it down Dead Man's Curve yet, either, Hoover."

Eddie pushed his face close to Skate's. Skate had never been this close to Eddie. He'd never looked as deeply into those shallow blue eyes. The part that wasn't blue was very red, he noticed. And Eddie's eyes had circles under them, as if he wasn't sleeping either. His normally pig-pink skin was pale. In spite of pig-nostrils and pig-eyes, Eddie didn't look like himself. He didn't look like a pig.

He looked like a sick pig.

"Back off, bacon-breath," said Skate. "When you make it down the Curve, then you can talk."

Eddie's little pig eyes got smaller. A little red flame seemed to leap up in them. Startled, it was Skate who stepped back.

Eddie grinned. His grin hadn't changed. It wasn't a pig grin. It was a grin that made a pig look good.

"I'll make it. I'll leave wheel marks on your face, McGraw. It takes a special talent to make Dead Man's

Curve. Special talent that you haven't got. Only some-one like me can get it."

Now Eddie stepped back. He raised his voice. "I'm gonna beat you tomorrow night, McGraw. I'm gonna leave skid marks down your back. You're gonna be a dead man, up on Dead Man's Curve."

CHAPTER
11

Halloween Day.

Skate woke up. He didn't remember falling asleep.

It was still dark outside. *Maybe I've only been asleep for a little while*, he thought. He felt tired and thirsty. He couldn't remember his dreams, but he was sure they had been weird ones.

He decided he didn't want to go back to sleep. He sat up and checked his clock. As he watched, the numbers rolled over from 11:59 P.M. to 12:00 A.M.

Halloween. It was official.

Something caught his eye. His skateboard. He'd left it out the night before propped against his desk. But the board wasn't propped against the desk now. It was sitting on the floor.

Skate frowned. Had it fallen? Was the sound of the board sliding down onto its wheels what had made him wake up?

Then his board moved.

Skate blinked.

His board wheeled slightly forward again. Noise-lessly.

I don't believe this, thought Skate.

He tried to get up, but he couldn't move. A puff of cold air made the curtains billow out.

The curtains? He hadn't left his window open.

Then Skate realized that his board was glowing in the dark. Faintly. But definitely.

Skate closed his eyes, then opened them. He swallowed hard.

His board was moving again. The wheels spun hypnotically. Silently. Faster. Faster.

His board was headed for the closed door of the bedroom. In another minute it was going to crash. In another minute it was going to commit skateboard suicide.

With a hoarse cry Skate somehow managed to lunge out of bed, The blanket was wrapped around his feet and seemed to tug him backward. He kicked wildly, did a belly flop onto the middle of his bedroom floor, and made a grab at his board.

He heard himself grunt as he caught the tail of it. For a moment the board actually pulled against his grip. It glowed more brightly, burning his fingers. Then the nose flipped up, and Skate let go.

Lying on his stomach in the middle of the room, he

watched his skateboard kick up onto its back wheels, shoot straight along the door to the ceiling, and turn a complete flip.

It started to fall.

As it fell, the glow left it.

Skate made another belly lunge across the floor. He got his hands under his board just before it landed, slamming his fingers with bone-crunching speed against the floorboards. He lay there, clutching it, feeling his fingers throb, breathing hard.

"Ouch!" he muttered. He held on. And waited.

Nothing happened. At last he lowered his board gently to the ground, wheels up. No point in taking any more chances.

He lay there for a long time, his burned, throbbing fingers pressed against the cool wood of the floor. At last a breeze from the open window roused him.

The open window. He hadn't opened the window. What was going on?

Eddie, thought Skate. *Eddie's behind all this. But how?*

He couldn't figure it out. It was creepy. It didn't make sense. But one thing he knew for sure—if he hadn't caught his board, its nose-first landing on the floor could have splintered it.

He'd seen it happen to other boards. He'd crunched one of his own ex-boards in a failed attempt to invent a new air spin. He could still hear the sound of the wood grinding into sawdust and matchsticks.

At last Skate rolled over and got up, keeping a close watch on his board. He eyed it for a moment, then picked it up. He walked to the window and shut it.

The moon was just going down. A nearly full moon. The next night the moon would be full.

Halloween night.

From his window on the second floor of his house, he looked down the street. Nothing moved. It was a bright and peaceful night.

As he turned away from the window, the clock rolled over from 12:00 to 12:01.

The whole thing had only taken one minute.

He took his skateboard and put it carefully on the bed next to him and put his hand on top of it. He didn't know what was going on, but he wasn't taking any chances.

He realized that he was shaking.

I'm scared, thought Skate.

It was going to be a bad Halloween.

"Trick or treeeeeeat!" Mrs. McGraw opened the door. "Aren't you cute!" she cried. She held out a bowl of miniature chocolate bars. "One each, now," she said.

The witch shoved the skeleton and took two.

"Ohhhh, a wicked witch," said Mrs. McGraw. The four trick-or-treaters giggled, and Mrs. McGraw gave the bat, the Ninja Turtle, and the skeleton an extra candy bar too. Then she waved at their neighbor, standing at the end of the front walk as the four kids ran back toward him.

"Look at meeee!" Skate's little sister came skipping down the hallway, waving a wand. She had silver wings attached to her back and was wearing a crown.

Skate rolled his eyes. "Cute," he said.

"I'm the Tooth Fairy," his sister told him importantly.

"Yeah," said Skate. "I could see that."

"Skate," said his mother warningly.

"Can we go now, Mommy, can we?" Christine was dancing around the hall in excitement.

"Just let me get my jacket." Skate's father was coming down the hall after Christine.

A moment later his father was headed out the front door, holding his little sister's hand. "Ooooh, look, Daddy," he heard her say. "It's Big Bird!"

His mother closed the door. "You used to be that little," she said to Skate. "Remember that cowboy outfit you had? You looked so adorable—"

"Mom," said Skate.

"Well, you did," said his mother. She ruffled Skate's hair. Skate ducked.

"I gotta go," said Skate.

"You and Park behave tonight," said his mother. "And don't forget you have to be back tomorrow morning by ten A.M. to stay with Christine."

Skate nodded. Normally he would have argued with his mother about having to baby-sit on a Saturday morning, especially the Saturday morning after Halloween, when his little sister was bound to be major cranky from sugar overload. But somehow he didn't even expect to be around the next day.

"Aren't you going to wear a costume?" asked his mother, surprised.

"Uh, it's in my pack," said Skate. He picked up his skateboard, and his mother looked down at it and frowned. "Skate," she began.

Just then the doorbell rang. She opened it. A big scarecrow and a tiny kid with puppy-dog ears and whiskers painted on her face stood there.

"Ooooh," crooned his mother.

"See ya, Mom," said Skate, slipping quickly out the door.

He walked out into a neighborhood filled with miniature ghouls and goblins, shrieking witches and giggling cats. Taller figures emerged from the shadows from time to time, shepherding the trick-or-treaters up and down the streets.

Skate walked through them without even noticing them.

He did notice the moon, though. It was just beginning to rise. It was full and yellow. And he didn't like the way it looked at all.

CHAPTER
12

"He's not coming!" crowed Eddie Hoover.

"He is too," said Vickie. "It's not midnight yet, Eddie."

"Skate is a chicken, Skate is a chicken," Eddie began to chant.

Vickie put her hands on her hips. "Oh yeah? Well, you sound like a chicken yourself, Eddie. I mean, why are you so glad that Skate's not here yet? Are you afraid of losing the contest? Afraid this is the only way you can win?"

"I'm not afraid!" Eddie almost shouted. "I can't lose." His voice sounded almost hysterical. He waved his arms wildly. "I can't! I won't!"

But Eddie wasn't looking directly at Vickie as he spoke. He was looking past her. Toward the graveyard past her shoulder, down the hill.

It gave Vickie the creeps. Forcing herself not to act like Eddie was weirding her out, she turned slowly.

Nothing was there.

"He's here," Eddie said dully.

"Skate?" Vickie turned back around and peered down the hill. She didn't see anyone.

"Where?" she asked Eddie.

Eddie didn't answer. He swallowed hard. He shook his head.

Then Vickie saw the figure at the bottom of the hill. "See?" she said to Eddie. "I told you Skate would be here."

Skate wasn't the only one there. Somehow half the school seemed to be headed toward the top of Skateboard Hill—the half that wasn't already waiting at the top.

How had everybody gotten out on Halloween at midnight without their parents knowing? Even perfect Polly Hannah! Vickie's eyes widened. "Polly, what are you doing here?" she asked.

"Shhh," said Polly, without offering any explanation at all. She walked past Vickie and stood next to Maria Medina at the top of the hill.

"It's about time, McGraw," said Eddie.

Skate didn't answer.

"Hurry up," someone said.

"Ready, McGraw?" Eddie sneered.

Skate nodded.

"We need to agree on some rules," said Park Addams, a classmate who had come up the hill just behind Skate.

"I'll judge," said Roy, stepping forward.

"Hah," said Vickie, surprising herself. But then, speaking to Roy wasn't the same as speaking to Skate.

Eddie said, "Who needs rules? The first person to make it down Dead Man's Curve wins."

"Are you racing?" asked Vickie.

Skate frowned. Eddie said, "Yeah."

Park said, "No."

Eddie frowned now. "Why not?"

"Hurry *up!*" Vickie recognized Polly's peevish voice.

"What about you do it three times?" Vickie suggested. "The person who makes it the most times wins. That way getting down the hill isn't just dumb luck. It proves who's the better skateboarder."

"I don't need three tries to prove I'm better," said Eddie.

"You don't think you can make it three times?" asked Vickie.

"What does McGraw want?" asked Roy.

Skate hadn't even been listening. He turned slowly from his contemplation of the dark curve below and played the words back in his head. He nodded. "Three times."

Park said, "And if no one makes it in three tries,

then you do a sudden-death duel. Side by side, all the way down. If you both make it, then the first person down wins."

Eddie laughed.

It was a creepy laugh.

"I'll judge the finish line," said Vickie. "The fence-post at the corner of the graveyard at the bottom of the hill."

She expected Eddie to protest. But he only jerked his head at Roy.

"Me too," said Roy.

Park flipped a coin. Eddie won the toss.

"Losers first," said Eddie.

Vickie groaned inwardly. Now Eddie would have the last chance. She looked toward Skate. But she couldn't tell whether he cared or not.

"Let's go," said Roy. He started walking rapidly down the hill.

Vickie looked toward Skate. "Good luck," she said.

Skate raised his eyes slowly from his contemplation of his skateboard. Had he heard her?

He nodded.

Feeling a little better, Vickie headed down the hill to join Roy.

The moon had risen high in the sky. In the bright, steady silver light, the faces of the crowd turned toward Skate and Eddie. Some of the kids were in costumes. Some were huddled in jackets.

As Skate lined his board up, a needle-sharp wind began to blow up the hill. It felt like an icy fingernail against his face.

Skate looked down the hill. He could see the boulders that marked the entrance to Dead Man's Curve as clearly as if it were day. A few of the kids lined either side of the road above the boulder. But no one had ventured all the way to the Curve.

Far below, he saw Vickie and Roy stop. They raised their arms and waved.

"Reaaady," came Roy's voice.

"Reaady," echoed Vickie.

Skate took a deep breath. He put his foot on his board. He leaned into the wind and took off.

He'd never boarded at night. Never this late. He crouched forward. His eyes watered in the cold wind.

The boulders on either side of the entrance to the Curve leaped up out of nowhere. The road seemed to be made of glass.

How fast was he going?

Every muscle in his body tensed, screaming for him to stop. He pushed himself forward.

He was through the boulders.

And then, with a little jerk, as if it objected, his board slipped from beneath his feet.

He wiped out.

"McGraw! You okay?" came Park's voice.

Skate took a deep breath and sat up. His board was just out of reach, He reached over and grabbed it.

It was fine.

"I'm okay!" he shouted, and got up to try again.

Eddie shot past him while he was walking back up the shoulder of the hill.

He heard the wipeout as he reached the top. And Eddie's unearthly howl of rage.

Skate put down his board and waited.

At last Eddie appeared. He was unsteady on his feet. His face looked bleached white in the moonlight.

"You all right, Hoover?" Skate asked in spite of himself.

"That wasn't supposed to happen," Eddie muttered, almost to himself.

With a shrug Skate planted his foot on the board again.

The second ride was faster than the first. Smoother.

And when he crashed right at the edge of the bridge, he crashed twice as hard.

"Skate?" Vickie's voice floated up to him.

"Yeah, no problem," he managed to call out. Was the ground harder on Dead Man's Curve or what?

He stood up. Picked up his board. Walked back up the hill.

Eddie waited until Skate got to the top this time before he started down. Then he was gone, kicking off wildly. His board careened, then settled. He shot through the boulders in an incredible blur.

"NOOOOOO!" screamed Eddie. And they heard his empty board clattering over the stones.

"Hoover?" shouted Park.

"Shut up!" Eddie screamed.

As he came back up the hill, Skate saw that the fall had ripped the leg of Eddie's jeans.

"You okay?" asked Skate.

"Quit stallin'," Eddie snarled.

Skate looked down the hill. The wind was colder than ever now. He bent over and checked his shoelaces. His knee pads. He adjusted his helmet.

He pushed off.

The wind cut through him like a knife. He couldn't breathe. The wheels of his board made a keen humming noise against the road. Or maybe it was the wind in his ears.

He realized that he'd gone through the boulders. He was coming onto the bridge.

He leaned. He tried to turn.

But he was out of control. The nose of his board was pointed straight for the railing. He was going to crash through it and out into the darkness and down into the deep, rock-filled water below.

He ground down hard on the tail of his board. He heard it bump protestingly over the boards of the bridge. The nose turned slightly. He stuck out his foot and jammed it against the railing and fell backward. As he fell, he instinctively reached down and grabbed the tail of the board.

For a moment he thought he'd lost it. For a moment he thought his board was going to leap through the railing and into the dark and down.

He landed on his back with a thump that knocked all the wind out of his chest. He hit his elbow so hard that he knew he was going to have a bruise even through his elbow pads.

But he had his board. He was holding it, barely, between the tips of his thumb and two fingers.

Gingerly he pulled it back. In spite of the abuse it seemed okay. With a silent apology to it, he sat up.

" . . . Okay?" Park shouted.

"Yeah," he answered.

He got up and walked back up the hill.

If Eddie made it now, Skate would lose.

He expected Eddie to make some nasty remark as he reached the top of the hill. But Eddie didn't even look in his direction. Instead he stared downhill as if he were puzzled.

"Eddie?" said Park.

"Yeah, all right," said Eddie.

He took off at the speed of light. *Or of dark*, thought Skate.

"Good run," said Park, coming up to stand beside Skate.

Skate nodded, his eyes on Eddie. *Please don't make it*, he thought. *I'd give anything if you wouldn't.*

He looked down and frowned. His board suddenly felt warmer in his hands.

Okay, he thought, *I lied. I wouldn't give anything for Eddie to lose. Especially not you, okay?*

Then he thought, *I can't believe I'm apologizing to my skateboard. I'm losing it. I'm losing my mind.*

When he looked up, Eddie had disappeared between the boulders. A moment later he flashed out of the bridge and banked toward the Curve.

Skate's heart sank.

"He's gonna make it!" someone shouted.

"No," whispered Skate.

Eddie kept going. Somehow. It wasn't style and it wasn't talent, but he was still standing up.

"Nooo," breathed Skate again.

And Eddie wiped out. At the top of the last, worst curve, his board shot straight up over the back edge. Eddie's arms flailed. His body twisted. Somehow he managed to stay on and bring the nose back around.

But he couldn't get back around with it. Arms still windmilling, he fell back into the middle of the road with an earthshaking crash.

"Somebody's in big trouble," said Polly's voice. "He's dead, for sure."

"He's not dead," said Maria Medina in disgust. "If he was, we'd smell him starting to rot already."

"You are so gross," Polly began.

Skate stopped listening. The figure in the road moved.

Another figure ran up from the finish line toward it.

"Leave me alone!" Eddie shouted. "I'm fine!"

Roy stopped, then turned and walked back down the hill.

Eddie got up slowly, slowly. He seemed to be looking around. He picked up his board and began to make his way back up to the top of Skateboard Hill.

Skate's heart began to pound.

Neither one of them had made it.

Now it was time for the sudden-death race.

Sudden death on Dead Man's Curve.

CHAPTER

13

Eddie didn't look good. His jeans were ripped. One of his knee pads was down around his ankle. He walked as if he hurt.

Skate wondered if he looked as bad as Eddie.

The students stepped back as Eddie walked by on his way up the hill. But Eddie didn't seem to notice. He kept looking over his shoulder.

As he got closer, Skate could hear Eddie muttering. But whatever Eddie was saying was caught up in the cold wind and blown away.

Skate checked his board. The wheels were working as they should. He checked the grip tape on the top of his board. He checked his shoelaces again.

Eddie lined up beside Skate. He was still muttering.

"Go get 'em, Skate!" shouted Maria.

That seemed to snap Eddie out of it. He raised his head with a jerk. He turned to look at Skate. His eyes narrowed. He thrust his head forward until he and Skate were helmet to helmet.

"It didn't work the first three times," he snarled. "But so what. This time, Skate, your board is *mine*."

Eddie's eyes were truly crazed. Skate decided it was better not to argue. He stepped back, never taking his eyes off Eddie.

"Line up your boards," said Park. He cleared his throat. "McGraw, Hoover, line up your boards."

Eddie held Skate's eyes for a moment longer.

He's lost it, thought Skate.

Then Eddie bent over with a grunt and dropped his board on the road.

Park cupped his hands and shouted down the hill, "READY?"

Vickie and Roy waved their arms.

"Yo!" shouted Roy.

"Ready!" shouted Vickie.

Eddie straightened up. He turned to survey the hill behind him.

But he wasn't looking at the crowd of students standing there. He was looking beyond them.

He turned. He smiled. The smile made him look worse than ever.

"Ready," said Eddie. "Eddie's ready."

"Me too," said Skate. He heard his voice crack.

Someone snickered.

Eddie just kept smiling.

Skate began to sweat.

"Okay," said Park. "I'll raise my right arm. When I drop it, and say 'Go,' take off."

Park raised his arm.

The crowd grew silent.

Skate could feel his heart beating. Without warning his teeth began to chatter.

Had Eddie somehow gotten bigger? Skate could feel Eddie's enormous bulk beside him. He felt as if Eddie were looming over him. He was barely able to keep himself from turning to look.

Concentrate, he told himself. *Concentraaaa—*

"GO!" shouted Park. A roar broke from the crowd.

Skate took off with everything he had. He felt his board seem to come to life beneath him, the way it did sometimes when he made memorable runs. His confidence came surging back.

Then he realized that Eddie was right beside him. Eddie's shadow stretched endlessly out on the ground before them. Skate's shadow looked puny beside it.

Skate crouched down for extra speed.

Eddie crouched down too.

The two of them shot between the boulders wheel to wheel. The darkness on the other side was bitter cold. The wind began to howl.

Skate felt it strike him like a blow, almost rocking him out of balance. But his board stayed steady beneath him.

Wheel to wheel they banked the first section and headed for the bridge.

Behind them, for just a moment, Skate heard people shouting. Ahead of him, for just a moment, he saw two figures waving their arms.

Then the bridge took his whole attention.

Their front wheels hit the planks at exactly the same time. Skate had never gone so fast on his board in his life. He'd never boarded so well. He wanted to shout with joy.

He wanted to scream with fear.

They were through the bridge. They dropped out of sight of the crowd behind them. The worst section of Dead Man's Curve was ahead, just over a nasty hill.

Their momentum carried them up the hill and into the curve. Now they were out of sight of the finish line below.

Skate had never made it this far before.

Someone was shouting. Screaming. Howling.

Skate crouched lower. Eddie's shadow on the road beside him began to flail its arms.

Eddie's gonna go, thought Skate. *He's gonna wipe out and take me with him.*

Desperately he looked over at Eddie.

Eddie looked bad. Really bad. His mouth was open. His helmet was askew. He was punching the air with his fists. He stooped and ducked and twisted his body. He was turning into a human pretzel.

How is he doing that? Skate thought in amazement. *No way he can stay on his board.*

Eddie's back arched. He threw his arms wide.

And Skate realized that he and Eddie weren't alone on Dead Man's Curve.

Ben Marrow was back.

The three of them shot over the top of the hill and hung in the air.

Skate felt the ground rise to meet his wheels. Felt it, but didn't see it.

He couldn't take his eyes off Ben Marrow.

Because Ben wasn't the smooth and excellent skateboarder he had appeared to be. He wasn't a thrasher in hiding, perfecting new and wonderful tricks.

And he definitely wasn't Olympic material.

If Eddie looked bad, Ben looked worse. In fact Ben looked dead.

Very dead.

Ben Marrow was a skeleton in thrasher's clothing.

His clothing fluttered in terrifying tatters in the breeze. His white skull glistened in the moonlight. His shirt was made of moldy rags. His jeans were dirt encrusted. Bony toes protruded from his shoes.

Ben Marrow turned his head and met Skate's horrified gaze. The skeleton's jaw dropped on its hinges. Little flames burned in his empty eye sockets. He threw back his head and began to laugh. Horribly. Soundlessly.

They banked the curve. Eddie twisted frantically, trying to guide his board away from Ben Marrow's. But it was useless.

Eddie turned to Skate. His mouth opened. "Help mmmeeee!" he cried.

CHAPTER
14

"Helppppp!"

Eddie pointed to his feet. Skate realized the awful truth. Eddie wasn't doing amazing skateboard tricks. He was out of control. He couldn't stop. He couldn't get off his board. His feet were stuck to it.

"Helppppp," the skeleton mocked, its teeth chattering. It threw back its head and laughed loudly. Then it reached one long bony hand out and put it on Eddie's shoulder.

Eddie shrieked. Then he seemed to grow smaller. And smaller.

Eddie's board edged ahead of Skate's.

They came out of the curve, and smoke spun up from Ben Marrow's wheels. Sparks icepicked holes in the dark.

Eddie was going to win. But he wasn't going to be

around to enjoy his victory. He was about to take the ultimate skateboard ride to the dark side.

Unless Skate could help.

With every ounce of strength he had, Skate threw himself sideways. He popped a wheelie and took to the air. He crossed in front of Eddie and shoved Eddie back with all his might as he did so.

A look of surprise crossed Eddie's face.

Skate careened into Ben Marrow.

A truly bony elbow caught him in the ribs.

And Eddie flipped backward off his board.

The skeleton turned to look back over its bony shoulder. Then it turned its skull to face Skate.

Skate stomped down on the tail of his board and got back in balance.

The last curve loomed ahead.

Ben Marrow grinned a toothy grin. He reached out for Skate.

"NO WAY!" shouted Skate. "CATCH ME IF YOU CAN."

He threw himself forward and took the curve on two wheels. He snaked Ben twice, zigzagging in front of him and cutting him off. He skateboarded with everything he had. He cut back across from his two-wheel flight up the far bank of the curve and slammed his board into Ben's.

Ben made another grab at Skate.

He missed.

But now all that was left was a straight stretch of road.

How could Skate outrun a skeleton?

He bent forward. He looked down at his board. *No one,* he thought, *no one gets my board.*

The smell of smoke filled the air. The wind howled. He couldn't breathe. He couldn't see.

He felt the brush of bony fingers against his shoulder.

And then he flashed over the finish line.

Behind him he heard a horrible sound, like a thousand bones being ground to dust. A cloud of bloodred smoke surrounded him as he tried to slow down. The image of Ben Marrow hovered beside him for a millisecond, the skull's empty eyes blazing evil fire, the teeth grinding together in unearthly rage.

Then it shattered.

Skate dropped his foot on the ground beside his board and dragged it hard. Gradually his board slowed down. He ended his ride down Dead Man's Curve in a big easy loop in the old parking lot.

He realized he was alive. And that he was facing Graveyard School. He half expected Basement Bart to come running out.

But the school stayed dark and still.

Maybe Halloween was a special holiday for Bart,

thought Skate. He wasn't thinking clearly. He was still numb. A voice in his ear brought him back to his senses.

"You won!" screamed Vickie. She was running along beside him. "You won! You won!"

Skate stopped. He unfastened his helmet. He bent and picked up his board.

It was still in one piece. "Good work," he said softly.

He looked up at Vickie. "You won," she repeated, her hands on her hips, watching him.

He nodded. How much had Vickie seen?

"You beat Eddie," said Vickie.

They stood for a long moment. *If she saw it,* thought Skate, *she's going to say I told you so.*

But Vickie surprised him. "You beat Eddie," she repeated. She grinned. "And you beat Ben Marrow."

"Hey!" Roy shouted. He was hurrying toward them, holding Eddie's board, while Eddie walked painfully along just behind. "Hey! What happened?"

"Where'd you go?" demanded Vickie.

"I heard Eddie shout and I figured he'd wiped out. I took a shortcut up the hill to help him," said Roy, panting.

"Skate won," said Vickie. "In case you hadn't noticed."

Students were pouring down the hill now. "What happened?" shouted Park.

"Skate won!" shouted Vickie.

Cheers broke out.

"Here come your fans," said Vickie.

The crowd flowed down the last section of the curve and parted to form a semicircle around Eddie and Skate and Vickie and Roy.

"We demand a rematch!" said Roy. "Skate cheated. He pushed Eddie. He—"

"No."

The word shocked Roy into speechlessness.

"No." Eddie shook his head. He held out his board. "It's yours," he said to Skate. "This part of the deal I keep."

Then he turned and walked away. The crowd parted silently to let Eddie by.

Roy stood there in disbelief a moment longer. Then he called, "Hey, Eddie, wait for me. Eddie!" He disappeared into the night after Eddie.

"Good work," said Park. Cheers and laughter erupted. For a long time the students milled around, thumping Skate on the back, congratulating him, congratulating themselves for seeing the big event.

Suddenly Polly whined, "I have to get home."

As if it were a signal, the crowd melted away, still murmuring congratulations.

Park was the last to go. "The back window, remember," he told Skate. "See you in a little while."

Skate and Vickie were left alone at the foot of Dead Man's Curve.

"Awesome ride," said Vickie.

"Yeah," said Skate. "The ride of my life."

He turned and started walking back up the Curve. Vickie fell silently into step beside him. When they reached the bridge, Skate raised Eddie's board up high.

It shone beautifully in the moonlight. It was a master board, a work of art, the most perfect board Skate had ever seen.

And it felt strangely warm in his hands. Wickedly warm.

Too hot for him to handle.

He drew his arm back and launched the board into the night beyond the railing of the bridge. It flashed hypnotically as it spun through the air. Then it dropped like a stone. As it hit the water below, an eerie flash of flame spurted up for a moment and then was gone. A sound of hissing, like steam off boiling water, rose from the stream.

Then the night was still.

"Hey, feel that?" said Vickie. "The wind stopped blowing."

They walked back home without talking, trailing through the empty streets past jack-o'-lanterns lit by dying candles. At Vickie's house she said, "I left the back door open."

Skate nodded. "Told my parents I was staying over at Park's. He left his window open."

They stood quietly for a moment. *She's going to say I told you so,* thought Skate. *Now she'll say it.* That was okay. She'd earned it.

But all Vickie said before she turned and headed around the side of her house was, "Well, maybe things can get back to normal now."

CHAPTER
15

Eddie didn't come to school for a few days.

"He's feeling kinda beat up," Roy explained to anyone who would listen. If Skate was anywhere in sight, he always added a dirty look, just for Skate.

Skate didn't mind.

He kept doing what he'd always done. Skateboarding. Dreaming of a skateboard event in the Olympics. Baby-sitting. Doing his homework when he had to.

Eddie remained a bully. His first day back he reduced a third-grader to tears and then laughed as Mr. Lucre marched him off to the principal's office.

"Eddie's tough," said Roy admiringly.

Nobody argued. Most people were still afraid of Eddie Hoover.

But Eddie avoided Skate and Vickie. He showed no interest in skateboarding. He didn't want to talk about it, didn't want to hear about it.

He announced that he wanted a new challenge. Maybe he'd learn to play chess.

"You'll kill 'em, Eddie," said Roy. "Before you can say checkmate."

Skate and Vickie kept practicing their skateboard moves up on Skateboard Hill. But they never took the turn down Dead Man's Curve. And they never stayed up on the hill after the sun went down.

The cold wind had started to blow off the graveyard again.

And once, just once, when they'd stayed there just a little longer than usual, something made Skate look back as they took the long road home.

He stopped. He pointed. "Vickie," he said.

Vickie turned. She stopped too. She looked in the direction Skate was pointing.

Then the two of them took off for home as fast as they could go.

Behind them, etched against the darkening sky, a skeleton on a Day-Glo neon skateboard was doing 360-degree reverse flips high in the air above the graveyard on Skateboard Hill.

Fill in the blanks and create your own gruesome ghost story!

The Haunted Classroom

Weird things have been happening in our _____
                                            (school subject)

class. I think it may be haunted by a _____.
                                          (object)

I first discovered this when my teacher, _____,
                                             (name of person)

turned to write on the black board. The lights went out.

Suddenly a big _____ _____ appeared
                  (texture)   *(object)*

over the teacher's head. My best friend, _____,
                                             (person)

screamed like a _____. My worst enemy,
                   (type of animal)

_____, jumped up and started to _____.
   (person)   *(action)*

Everybody laughed, even though it was scary. Then the

lights came back on. "_____," our
                          (phrase)

119

teacher shouted. "Settle down!" Our teacher turned

around, and much to our horror had turned into a

———————————— . But that didn't prevent our teacher from
     (animal)

giving us a ten-page homework assignment on

——————————————. And that was the *scariest* part of all!
(something boring)